Roeing Oaks

Roeing Oaks

KRISTINA EMMONS

ISBN 978-0-615-32267-4

History—Great Britain—Victoria, 1837-1901—Fiction

Cover design by Amaniac Design

Printed and bound in the United States of America, Lulu Enterprises

To my husband and our children
with all my love

Chapter One

As I lay with my eyes closed to the glow of dawn, I wondered if this news meant that I was a bastard child. Well, I was no longer a child; I was nearly a woman, yet the word *bastard* would not leave my consciousness. It prodded me like accusing fingers, smoldered within me like reddened coals. It may not have mattered, given my lowly station: the dregs of society have no shade of variance; they are but dregs. Still, this brought me no comfort. I would wake Mother and ask her to explain it, though we'd already spent much of the night discussing—her secret.

I opened my eyes and found Mother gone from the opposite end of our bunk; neither was she elsewhere in our single room cottage. The teacups, dirtied from our long night, rested on the table beside the pot that should by now be filled with fresh tea if we were to get our journey underway.

I roused myself.

As I descended the bunk I brushed against the mantel, knocking the newly arrived letter to the floor. For a moment I stood looking down at it. I had a thought to pitch it into the waning embers in the hearth. Instead, I lifted it to its original resting place and took a step backwards. What if it had never come? Would Mother have ever told me?

I shivered and wrapped a shawl about my shoulders, laced up my boots so that I may go outside to find her. As I did I caught sight of my black gown hanging beside the bunk. I took it from its hanger to fold it and place it in the carpet bag. The bag sat beside the cottage door, threads fraying at the edges like straying sheep. I walked over to it. I saw that Mother's things were already in it, her own black gown included.

At that moment the door opened, revealing Mother, her arms laden with kindling. She took pains to close the door noiselessly. When saw me, she averted her eyes. At once I understood why she made effort to avoid me.

"You would truly leave me behind?" With no response, I continued. "Shouldn't I be afforded a chance to meet my own kin? Never mind that after a lifetime you at last decide to tell me the truth!"

Mother piled the lot of wood beside the hearth as I spoke, then wearily threw a branch among the embers.

"Kate, if not for that letter I may never have told you."

My fears were confirmed. She tidied the pile of kindling. "Your grandmother will be expecting only myself. Besides, we've only enough train fare for one, and you know Mr. Boyle depends on us to keep the farm."

"But Mother! It's nearly March. It isn't even growing season. Our chores can endure a few days neglect, and Joseph, he already minds the livery. Surely he can see to the milking as well for a few days. Mr. Boyle will understand," I urged.

Mother glanced sideways at me. We both knew well that Mr. Boyle, our landlord and employer, would not understand. All her excuses were cover for what she knew I would not wish to hear.

"Kate, just as I never told you of my family before last night," she paused and turned her head from me, "they, too, are unaware of you."

I was stunned into silence.

"I never told them," she continued. "Alistair—he'd gotten to them all first. They never knew I carried his child, and they would not have trusted my words over his. God only knows what he said of me. All I am certain of is that I've been cut off. Utterly cut off." She sighed. "Ah, no good comes of dwelling on what cannot be changed."

How cruel was this Alistair Percy! The idea that I shared blood with him was revolting.

3

"My grandparents, they might have understood, if only you would have—" I offered.

Mother kept her eyes on the tea she was preparing. "It isn't so simple, Kate."

I balled up the black gown, still in hand.

Mother explained that the postmistress had been suspicious when the letter arrived at the Post Office, as it had been addressed to mother under the name Victoria Braithwaite-Percy, not Victoria Thurgood, as she was here known. It was a wonder it found its way into Mother's hands at all, but if anyone discovered that Thurgood was not our legal name—who knows what could become of us.

I grasped at anything that could be said to convince Mother to bring me along to Holmsbridge. At last I applied guilt.

"Mother, you owe this to me, and you owe them the explanation," I said as firmly as I dared.

She sighed and turned to face me with tired eyes.

"Holmsbridge is the estate I was raised on, and I know it well. If you come there will be stares and whispers, and the possibility of an encounter with your true father. Could you endure it? Could you withstand it if he publicly denies you?"

I nodded confidently, though my resolve was questionable.

"Gather your things then, but do not hold me responsible for the events to come. We will first notify Mr. Boyle."

From beneath her garments in the battered trunk, Mother retrieved a second carpetbag that I had never seen, and from an unused pitcher at the top of the hutch she fished out a mysterious roll of bills.

I resisted the urge to question her about it and gathered my things in silence.

THE EASTERN SUNLIGHT CAUSED our shadows to extend far before us. I hoped it was no omen of darkness to come. As we walked with our heads downcast, we watched as the tips of our boots peeped out from beneath the hems of our best dresses. Small clumps of crocus and hawthorn peeked out hither and thither from the half frozen ground. After the unusually severe winter we had just passed, I wondered if they would have returned again at all. If all fared horribly at Holmsbridge, I took heart that our old stand-bys, the daffodils and narcissi, would still arrive to cheer us.

When we had reached Mr. Boyle's estate, we set our bags on the doorstep and stood hunching, as much from the wind as from the prospect of a verbal assault. With great courage Mother grasped the lip of the brass lion that served as the door knocker. It was colossal in size, so as to intimidate, and its fierce expression was the mirror of the man that lived beyond it.

Through the door we heard footsteps approaching, much as the rumble of thunder precedes a storm. The door was swung open and we were met with a scowl. The head of Mr. Boyle's household carried out not only his orders, but his foul demeanor. "Yes?" she hissed.

"I must speak with Mr. Boyle at once," Mother demanded. Nelly shifted her weight and placed one hand on her meaty hip. "My father lays on his deathbed. We go this morning to Somerset," Mother said in her most official tone. If Nelly had known with whom she was speaking she would not hesitate to offer us every convenience; and beg Mother's forgiveness.

"Somerset, eh?" She narrowed her eyes. I suspected she hadn't the slightest idea where Somerset was located. Probably she had never set foot outside of our county in all her life. Nor had I. She puffed out her chest.

"Master's not accustomed to letting tenants off without advance notice. But he's gone to London for the week—won't be back till Tuesday." She leaned in as though divulging a secret. "Supposing you've made it back by then—" she waved her hand in dismissal.

What was this? I concluded it must be her own freedom from "the Master" that had her in benevolent spirits. Mother thanked her and explained that Joseph the livery man had

6

agreed to keep watch over the property. Nelly closed the door with a thud before Mother could finish her sentence.

With unspeakable relief we set off for Northampton Station.

Chapter Two

The clamour of Northampton Station was outside my realm of experience. In town at Hazel Grove, not even Sundays or public celebrations drew such a crowd. I was unaccustomed to brushing shoulders with complete strangers. The noise was deafening: shrills of small children, vendors shouting of their wares, young and old competing for headway in the great race to board the train in a timely fashion. I allowed Mother to pioneer our trail through it all beneath the enormous steel arches that stretched over the railway.

I had been to the station as a small girl to bid Earnest farewell, but everything had been different then. The station had only just been built, and word was still getting around to the country population that trains were an efficient and safe mode of travel. As we now neared the great beast that would take us to Somerset I thought of him, how he had stepped into its belly and vanished forever. In my stupor I missed a step while boarding.

"Attention!" a man with a heavy accent shouted contemptuously from behind me. When I realized he was a Frenchman I suddenly felt cultured. I smiled and was returned a glare. It was my first encounter with a foreigner, save the Micks, which weren't really foreigners at all.

As we were seated inside the train, I studied the crowd outside through the windows. The cars behind us were for those riding third class. We were fortunate to be riding second class that day. We had the benefit of sitting four across on benches, whereas those riding in third class were packed in like cattle. The passengers there appeared as worn as the clothing on their backs. Rightfully we belonged with them, but Mother's pride would not allow for the demotion. How had I neglected to take notice of the great depth of contrast between the classes before that day?

I watched as ladies strolled along with fancy parasols slung over their gloved wrists. They wore shawls and wraps, and were clothed elegantly in yards of bright materials and patterns I had never had the opportunity to touch, much less purchase. Trimmings of satin and lace seemed to proliferate out of their bodices and cuffs as shoots of ivy. On their heads were frilled bonnets or flowered ornaments, and interwoven in their well-styled hair were ribbons. Trailing them were ladies-in-waiting or child servants, and young men who, for a few coins, scampered about for the honor of bearing the great trunks holding what could only be guessed at.

The gentlemen donned top hats, capes and greatcoats, and held iron tipped walking sticks. Their hair was combed to perfection, their facial whiskers trimmed and styled with precision. One could see their reflection in the surface of their polished footwear.

Suddenly I felt seedy in my faded calico, the only decent garment I owned, and already a year past requiring replacement. Even among the second class passengers it was unattractive and antiquated. Why, there was not a fashionable thing about me! I pushed my worn carpetbag from view. Mother had surely purchased it used at market, and I was convinced my neighbors were eyeing it with disdain.

I turned to look at Mother, who was attractive even in her own faded calico. Her figure was perfection, and if not for her years spent labouring on the farm, her complexion would have been porcelain still. The worn straw hat she so staunchly insisted we don in the sun had done well to preserve her skin from patina. I admired her, and truthfully, I envied her eyes. I imagined that in her youth they sparkled as jade. Presently, they held the keenness of a cat and the presence of a magnate.

I watched as the last of the first class passengers boarded the plush cars reserved for them. A sickly lump formed in my stomach. Was this the face of my bloodline? No longer did I wish to be on that train.

"Kate, be strong. We will do this together." Mother said, sensing my agitation.

"How long have you kept a stash of money in the pitcher?" I asked when I could stave off my curiosity no more.

"Darling, every mother saves for her child. If you were to die suddenly there must be provision for the funeral."

"Funeral? That is the reason you were saving money? What of all the times we did without basic necessities? Each time I could have used a new undergarment or a frock, or a pair of decent boots?"

"You have seen enough tragedy to understand it is not uncommon to lose a child to sudden illness. It is my duty to provide a proper burial in that event. We are blessed to have survived the cholera outbreak when you were small. And what if I pass? Who would pay the expenses? Certainly not Mr. Boyle. He'd sooner have me thrown into a ditch than donate a penny toward a proper burial."

I blinked in disbelief. I had never considered such things, and upon reflection I realized the stash must have been what had gotten us through that winter when so many suffered without bread in the food shortages. I had newfound respect for Mother.

Kristina Emmons

The train lurched forward. I fought to keep from queasiness as I watched the passing landscape. I was quite obliged that, despite the circumstances, I was getting the opportunity to ride on a train! By the time we had reached Somerset even this held no relish, as the jerking motion of the train and the great speed at which we tore through the air took their toll on my body and my sensibilities.

I was utterly intimidated to learn during the ride that my maternal grandfather was a gentleman and the head of a banking empire, a gentleman in those days meaning a man in the gentry who could partake in the functions of upper class society. My birth father was a baron, which meant that he ranked at the lowest level of the nobility.

I imagined that meeting me could only incite in my grandparents a grave distaste. I reminded myself that it was they that penned us and not the reverse. There must be some hope of reconciliation.

At last we stepped from the train and onto the platform in Glastonbury Station, wearied from the journey. Before long we spotted a placard with Mother's name on it, held by an older gentleman with a large hooked nose. A butler, I assumed. Before Mother could speak the man asked her if she was Mrs. Braithwaite-Percy.

"Yes, it is I. Do you not recognize me, Reginald? It has been many years, yet I remember your face as clearly as the day

12

I saw you last." Mother grasped his wrist as one would that of an old friend.

"Madam," he said before bowing. He looked her over with distaste. I could see Mother's pain at his coolness. She casually removed her hand.

"Mrs.—Braithwaite," he continued, unsure of how to address her, "It is with regret that I inform you of your father's passing. It was only last evening that he took his final breath. Tomorrow he is to be buried."

Mother staggered as though whipped.

"It was inevitable," she said as she dabbed her eyes with a handkerchief. With heaviness she raised her head. "You must take me at once to my mother. I am sure there is much to arrange."

"Do not trouble yourself. Your sister Betina has been with your mother to comfort her and to see to the preparations."

Mother's eyes lowered. I was in awe at the harshness of his tone.

Reginald looked us over. "Shall the girl be coming along?" Mother nodded. "The carriage is this way." He turned and walked on without regard as to whether or not we followed.

After a silent carriage ride we found ourselves at Holmsbridge's gate at dusk. The scrolled iron structure was a formidable work of art, yet even more so was the estate that lay just beyond it. What had been a monstrosity to me in Mr.

Boyle's estate was eaten up by this colossus. The center jewel of the lush landscape was a sprawling abode, flanked by wonderfully manicured circular gardens. I could only imagine that in a few months when the flowers were in bloom it would transform into an Eden.

When the carriage stopped, we were met by two footmen that assisted us out of the carriage and carried our bags to the door. What contrast the fraying bags made against the entrance! I studied Mother's face as the footmen opened the carved door that towered so far above us that I had to strain my neck to see its top. In my youth I could not have ascertained the gravity she was feeling.

Inside the foyer, the mahogany staircase seemed to put on airs, loudly proclaiming its own grandeur like a vain peacock. But it had competition in the forest green marble flooring, for every footstep taken upon it sounded as a chorus of church bells. In its very essence, the manor was reminiscent of a cathedral, complete with a holy hush.

We were instructed by Reginald to wait for his return. He disappeared into an obscure entrance behind the staircase, his footsteps echoing along the way like faraway voices.

"It's dreadful quiet in here," I whispered to Mother after all sound had subsided. Even my whisper was magnified against the silence.

We heard Reginald approaching well before he was again seen.

"Madam will see you now," he said, and brusquely set off up the staircase. I was beginning to understand that whenever he turned and walked on we were meant to follow after him.

Chapter Three

I could no longer hear our footsteps as we ascended the stairs, only could I hear my heart beating as that of a trapped rabbit. I held to Mother's hand. It was cold and trembling. The blood seemed to have drained from her face as well. This only served to magnify my own nerves.

At last Reginald opened the door to a room and stepped inside. "Madam," he addressed the woman as he bowed and held his hands out to present Mother. His brow furrowed as he caught sight of me.

"Right this way," he whispered snippily into my ear.

"No," Mother said. "She will remain with me." Reginald looked me over with distaste before echoing off down the hallway.

I turned my focus to the woman before me. So this was my grandmother. She stood near the marbled hearth in her black mourning gown. Her head was respectfully covered in a black bonnet with a long crape veil, which she had pushed back, though her eyes and nose remained covered with black tulle. When she turned toward us, the diamond encrusted brooch over her left breast flashed in the firelight. I assumed it was a memento from my grandfather; else it would be vulgar to display it during mourning.

The Madam, as I shall heretofore call her, remained silent, and from her stony expression I could tell no emotion. It was Mother who spoke first.

"It hardly seems possible to be standing here just now." She walked up to her mother grasped her hands. "I imagine you are suffering greatly under the circumstances. I am here at your beck and call should you need anything of me."

The Madam leaned away from Mother's touch. She recovered her hands before addressing her daughter.

"Dear Victoria, everyone has their hour," she said in a gravelly voice. "Not far into the distance it will be mine. Won't you have a seat?" she said in a manner reserved for greeting a new acquaintance. She motioned toward a wing-back chair. Mother glanced at me before sitting, a glance that the Madam's eyes followed. I would learn quickly that nary a movement escaped her eye.

"Will your lady be staying? She *can* be dismissed, can't she?" I at last understood that I was being mistaken for a lady's maid, a handmaiden if you will.

Mother stroked her neck. "Yes, she may wait outside the door." With her eyes she communicated to me that I must exit immediately and without a fuss. I concealed my injury and obeyed, yet as I departed I kept the door slightly ajar so that I might eavesdrop.

"Mother, may we have a chat?" I heard the muffled voice say. "There is much to discuss, and I cannot pretend to imagine that we will cover it all, but—"

The Madam guffawed. "I hardly think now is the proper moment to have a chat. Your father is buried tomorrow and I've much on my mind. I think it civil of you to have come, though I suppose it could not be helped that your arrival was belated. You may visit the casket in the morning when you have rested. Have you no mourning clothes? I hardly know what to make of you, dressed so."

"I have brought a simple black mourning gown."

"Perhaps I will have one of the ladies bring an assortment of my own gowns for you to choose from; there will be need of adjustments. Good Lord, where has your figure gone? All your curves…"

From the hallway I imagined her assessing Mother's shape with repugnance.

"Alas, I must bid you good night. Reginald has had your—belongings—secured in the Blue Room. Your lady may stay in the servant's quarters. Be sure to have her in black on the morrow."

"Yes, of course. Good night, milady. Rest well." I heard Mother say quietly.

In seconds she was by my side again. She brushed past me and did not stop until we were in what was unmistakably the Blue Room. The draperies, bed coverings, carpets—all were blue of one shade or another.

Our carpet bags rested beside a table laden with fruits and pastries. My eyes grew in hungry anticipation. The luxury of fresh fruit at this time of the year, and pastries at any time of the year, was a great treat. I knew it wasn't proper to eat while Mother was in such a state, but I could not stop myself from reaching for an orange, imagining its sun-drenched tropical origins. As I did, we heard a rap at the door. A young lady's maid stood holding a black gown made of Henrietta cloth, its sleeves and neckline trimmed with black tulle.

"Madam has ordered a fitting for you, milady."

"Very well," Mother said, by now more than a bit disconcerted. She snapped at the maid and fidgeted during the fitting. "Do be sure to bring some polished boots if you can find any to fit my foot. I'm afraid these will simply not do. And do not neglect to bring a pair of black kid gloves. I have not had the liberty to purchase a new pair in good time. Madam would be furious to see me in a silk pair at first mourning. I shall expect them first thing."

I did not know what to make of this authoritarian facet of Mother. And her speech—so queenly! I stuffed my mouth with sumptuous pastry as I watched.

When the girl had gone I tilted my head in question. Mother threw her hands up in the air. "'Tis this, this place! It brings out the worst in me. Did you hear your grandmother? She hasn't the time for a chat! After all this time she hasn't the heart to give me the slightest length of slack. I wanted to explain, to tell her of you. Now I am not sure what I will do. And you should have seen the scorn in her eyes when she saw how I was dressed! I do wonder what rumors have been told of me."

"Cheer up! How can you be cross in such an exquisite room, and with pastries to devour! One bite and your countenance will brighten as the sun. I have had several and behold my joy." I twirled and dropped onto the massive four poster bed, sighing at its comfort.

Mother laughed. "True, indeed. A bite of pastry does do wonders for the countenance. That is one virtue your grandmother possesses—an appreciation for sweets. As for this room, it's one of the least lovely. The Violet Room is far grander! I will wager your Aunt Betina has been given the honor of staying there. Oh, to see her again! The viper! Tomorrow you must act as my buttress."

"But how can I? I don't see how it is I can attend the burial when the Madam does not know me."

"We shall pray. The Lord will reveal all to us."

"Surely you don't intend to send me to the servant's quarters to sleep?"

Mother laughed. "Of course not, dear. We will share the bed, as we always do. Hear me: tomorrow we will tell her. Good night, darling."

I climbed in beside her and pulled the blankets to my chin. "Sleep well." Moments later I was asleep.

The next morning I was loathe to awaken and dislodge my weary body from the marvelous bed. After sleeping on a thin woolen mattress all my life, the sensation of thick layers of down feathers and soft bedclothes beneath me was the embodiment of heaven. Mother's voice roused me at last, her commandments toward a lady-in-waiting as she helped her to dress. "It'll need a nip here. Oh, and another here." I opened my eyes begrudgingly to find Mother smoothing her skirts.

She was a vision! The black gown was ever so complementary to her figure, due mainly to the new corset she was wearing beneath it. This corset was not hopelessly falling to pieces as the one she normally kept for wearing to church, with bits of boning poking out here and there like the beaks of

21

newborn chicks as they peck through eggshells. This one was smoother than glass. And Mother's hair was arranged so wonderfully, swept back in sections that were brought together to form an intricate knotting that I'd never seen before. It was a far cry from the outdated chignon she and I normally wore.

When the lady had gone and I had donned my own plain black frock I willed myself to praise Mother, despite my envy.

"It's befitting?" she asked breathlessly, an after effect of the lacing of her corset. "Oh, it's dreadful of me to enjoy a mourning gown! But I haven't worn such fine craftsmanship for, well, decades, I suppose."

As Mother donned her gloves, I helped her fit a long veil to the back of her bonnet. Just then, a rap at the door startled us. In walked Reginald, in his arms a tray of breakfast fare. Just behind him, a young man carried a silver tea service.

"Good morning to you, madam," said Reginald to Mother. It was a statement more than greeting. After narrowing his eyes at me he signaled his companion to enter and set the tea tray on the table. As he turned I saw a tuft of white hair sticking out from the back of his head, giving him the appearance of a perturbed duckling. I dared not laugh aloud.

"I've only brought enough food for one," he said to Mother in accusation.

"Reginald, what is this?" Mother asked with her hand at her hip.

He motioned for the second man to exit the room before he spoke.

"Per Lady Braithwaite's request," he answered Mother and blinked, as if this should explain everything.

"Is there a particular reason she does not wish for me to take breakfast with her in the breakfast room?"

Reginald seemed disconcerted. "Madam is hosting a large group of people this morn, and she assumed you would be more comfortable dining privately. She left a note for you on the tray. As for your lady—"

As I was now standing beside the table that held the tray, I snatched up the note before anyone saw.

"You may now go, Reginald," Mother said. He straightened his back and exited.

I read the note quickly. It was a warning to Mother to keep herself hidden among the crowd. She was not to let on her identity.

"Let us be going then," she said as she walked toward the door. I decided it was not the time to relate what the note said. Besides, it seemed she had already perceived.

"Where? What about the food?" I protested. I had been lusting after it from first glance. Contrary to what Reginald had said, there was more than enough food for two.

"I've lost my appetite. We shall go to see the casket."

Chapter Four

Mother and I zigzagged through the manor, my stomach grumbling along the way. How long it took for us to reach the east end where the casket lay I do not know, I only knew that I would have never found my way back to the Blue Room unattended.

Of course our jagged route was by design. We were, after all, attempting to avoid being seen. When we reached the room that had been my grandfather's study, Mother paused at the door and sighed heavily.

"Let me pass a few moments with him. Will you wait here?" she asked. I nodded. A surprisingly short time after, she emerged with eyes rimmed red. "Go in and pay your respects," she whispered. Reluctantly, I entered.

I had never before seen a corpse. Walking into a room containing one was fearsome. Despite the floral displays about the room, I could smell the pungent odor of fleshly decay. The stillness of death engulfed me, and time itself seemed to arrest there amongst the potted jungle of lilies.

I needn't elaborate how awkward it was having my first meeting with my grandfather by way of a casket, yet oddly it was comforting to know his face. I looked with a measure of fondness upon his bald crown, and the grayed handlebar mustache that someone had taken the care to groom in what I imagined had been his customary style. His hands were manicured, yet not feminine, and there was an indentation in the fourth finger of his left hand where a ring had been secured for countless years. These were certainly not the hands of a field worker. For an instant I considered pushing open his eyelid to discover the colour of his eyes, then I shook myself. This bit of information I could ask of the living.

In all, I ascertained that he had been kind. I should have liked to have known him.

"Farewell, Grandfather Braithwaite," I whispered, choking on the words and feeling a trespasser as I said it. I hesitantly leaned over to touch his hand. The shock of his cold, lifeless skin against mine has never left me, and never again have I touched a corpse, save that of my own mother many years later.

I embraced Mother upon exiting the room. "What now?" I whispered. She sighed.

"Let us intercept your grandmother." She took my hand and escorted me on. I was short of breath upon reaching the dining room, for she walked speedily.

"Pardon me," Mother addressed a servant at the door. "Would you do me a grand favor and tell Madam Braithwaite I wish to speak with her just now?" The girl looked frightened.

"Milady, madam is not inclined to be interrupted during mealtimes."

"Do you know who I am? I am her daughter, and I wish to speak with her just now." The girl only looked at her with widened eyes.

Mother continued. "If you do not go in I will, and I assure you the Madam will be far more disturbed in that instance." The girl nodded her head and walked in stiffly, and just after we heard a set of angry footsteps approaching.

The fury in the Madam's eyes as she tossed back her black veil should have caused me to quiver, yet I felt my own fury rising within. I had inherited a streak of my grandmother's ire. She did not speak, but swept past us, cool breeze that she was, motioning with a flick of her hand that we follow her. Once in a separate chamber, she closed the doors behind us.

"Now what is the meaning of this?" she said, her voice controlled. This was the first good look I had gotten of her features. She was handsome, I thought, despite her taut expression and steely eyes. Above and below her eyelids the skin drooped, and wrinkles on either side of her eyes seemed to be groaning against the added weight.

"I apologize but I could wait no longer to speak with you," Mother began.

"Have you no respect for the dead?"

At this Mother could keep her composure no more. "The dead? What of when he was alive? Must you have waited until his death?"

"How *dare* you come into my home and speak to me so! *I* invited you here, remember that. When you are in my home you will behave with respect. If your father had not requested your presence…"

"Father? How long had he been requesting to see me? How long have you kept me away, Mother?"

"It is you who kept yourself away! I suggest you retreat at once, unless you wish to show yourself, Victoria, show yourself the daughter I raised! You are proving yourself to be quite the vulgar wench."

Mother gasped. She re-gathered herself and straightened. "I cannot leave this alone," she said with tears in her eyes. "This has transpired far too long and my name must be cleared. You will hear the truth for once! Mother, look upon your granddaughter. This is Katherine," she said as she pulled me forward. "Before you make your judgment, she is the child of Alistair Percy."

I felt myself shrink back at my grandmother's disbelieving, probing eyes.

"Well, can you deny his resemblance in her? I tell you it is God's honest truth!" Mother urged. The Madam turned away.

"Victoria, do you in your contempt expect me to believe that this sickly being is the offspring of Alistair Percy?" Her words were sharp like the snip of a scissors.

"Give her a few weeks of good food and diminish her worry and she'll be full of pluck. I can only imagine Alistair told you I had run off with some lover, some tycoon, and who knows what Betina has fed you. I ask you this, what proof or evidence did anyone offer you? I knew that attempting to convince any of you otherwise would prove unfruitful, for you have always been so fond of Alistair, and his charm is indeed compelling. This is the truth."

"Explain to me then. What is the truth according to Victoria?" The Madam asked with her back turned still.

Mother took a breath. "The truth is that the morning after telling Alistair that I was pregnant, he insisted we leave for London. He told me to dress casually, and before I could question him we were in the carriage and on our way. I scarcely had time to gather together a small bag of toiletries. In the carriage he remained silent. I never imagined where he could be taking me.

"Once in London he dismissed the carriage. He ushered me into a crawler cab, and instead of taking me to a park, we continued on until we were in a place I had never seen before. It was very common. You can't imagine the filth that filled the streets—dung and all! We left off at what I now know was the Smithfield meat market. There were throngs of people, throngs of cattle. The stench was unbelievable! Alistair gave me a look that I knew to mean I should not question him and firmly held to my arm. He pulled me through to a certain man, who after a private talk between them hung a rope loosely around my neck. A rope! I laughed, as it must have been a joke, but no." Mother stopped to wipe a tear from her eye. I welled up as well.

"I was led up to the auction block by that horrendous rope, up where the animals are displayed for sale, much to the amusement of the crowd. I stood there amongst the chaos as the auctioneer addressed the people. I don't know what he said. After, some of the men jeered and shouted their bids. I can't tell you how humiliated I was, how horrified. I looked to Alistair, who coldly stood by, insisting with his eyes that I play along. I tried to find explanation; perhaps he was trying to frighten me. It couldn't be real! When he was satisfied with the bidding I was led away to the winner. Alistair—he—he took the money and never looked back."

"Sold you!" The Madam scoffed. "A fairytale! Only commoners do it, and for sport, or so I hear. Do you truly expect me to believe this nonsense? You know how I can't abide dishonesty, and worse, theatre."

"I know it sounds preposterous. If he wanted me gone, why would he have done something so crude? I do not pretend to know the answers. There is so much to explain and we haven't the time now. By the grace of God there was a man passing that was filled with mercy, and not some greedy pig who wished to exploit me. Who knows in London where I would have ended up, with the all of the prostitution plaguing the city. I have been able to make something of a life for myself—just barely, but a life."

"How do you know the child is the fruit of Alistair Percy? Betina has said you told her you could not conceive. And now you claim another man bought you."

"Oh, Mother, why must you always believe Betina? She is a lover of all things theatrical, speaking of theatre. Alistair knows I was pregnant, and it's high time everyone stops falling bewitched by every word he speaks." Mother paced in the awkward silence that followed. "Perhaps it is best that we do not attend the burial," she offered.

The Madam raised her hand. "No, you will attend. I shall arrange for you a private carriage. Go, but make yourselves of no consequence. Remain in the back, and keep your heads down and your veils over your faces. Don't speak with anyone, not even Betina. Any accusation as grave as this begs investigation; you must stay on past the ceremony." She looked at me once more before pulling her heavy crape veil over her face and quitting the room.

"Well," I said with a gulp of relief.

"Do not speak! I'm shaking," Mother said as she held her hand over her heart.

"But Mother! She did not deny your words. Do you think she believes you?"

"Time will tell. I do wonder why she did not immediately run us out. Let us go await the carriage." I returned to the Blue Room to fetch my bonnet and gloves, and of course, a bite to eat before we went to our carriage.

We would later meet with good reason why the Madam might believe us.

Chapter Five

We did not attend the ceremony that was held in the parlour where the casket lay. Instead we awaited the funeral party in a carriage. Going unnoticed proved effortless enough, as we kept the shades drawn in our coach. From behind our shade I watched the hearse round the bend toward the main road, its over-sized canopy of ostrich feathers swaying to the rhythm of the horses, each with its own set of dancing feathers on their head. The other coaches followed behind to form an arc that reached a long distance before us and followed onto the road. My grandfather had surely been well esteemed to have drawn such a crowd to his funeral.

I turned to Mother.

"Mum, there is something I need to know about Father—I mean, Earnest."

"Hmm?" she murmured, her head leaning back and her eyes closed.

"Earnest. I have a memory of him. He was telling me a bedtime tale. I remember his voice was deep and gentle, and that I fell asleep in his arms. But what just occurred to me is that I never remember him talking so to you. And then I got to wondering—in all this mess, were the pair of you ever—ahem—consummated?"

Mother shot out of her restful stance like a frog over flame. "I beg your pardon?"

"Were the two of you consummated?"

"Well, I suppose I could have explained this. First of all, we never shared a bed. As you recall he always slept in the loft above the stables, unless the weather was not permitting. No, we weren't able to be married. There was no legal divorce from Alistair, at least none that I know of. I could not see being married before God to two men at once. Being sold is rare, but your grandmother is right. Normally commoners do it as a way to circumvent obtaining a divorce. Divorces cost more than many of them make in many years' time.

"The crowd serves as a witness to the separation. From what I have gathered over the years, the couple agrees to it, and it is a sport to put a piece of rope around her neck and put her on a block. The winning bidder is arranged beforehand, someone the wife is keen on being with—the crowd knows this.

Once the money is exchanged the new couple lives as though married, though in the eyes of the law they are unjustified.

"As for the wealthy, such behavior is scoffed at. It is naturally considered improper, which is why it is a mystery that Alistair would have considered doing it at all. I imagined the crowd around me thought I had agreed to it, and they were waiting for the highest bidder to make his appearance. Earnest sensed that something was wrong. I shall always love him for it stepping into my life that day to save us. He didn't ask to be walking by; he didn't ask to raise someone else's child for his own."

"If your marriage was legally dissolved would you have married him?"

"I don't suppose all this talk changes anything."

"It would help me a great deal to know if my mother loved my—father," I said, the word uncomfortably falling from my lips.

"The truth is I would have married him for our safety. But the love between us was brotherly love. It was respectful."

"Then it is good. Good that his life ended so that he didn't have to regret living with a sister and not a lover."

"Kate, tread lightly," Mother warned.

"It wasn't fair to him! And me? Did he love me?"

"Of course he loved you! The way he looked at you! His heart was *filled* with love for you! Don't you think I know how unfair it was for him? I even encouraged him to find himself a lover but he would not. He was a good man, bless his soul. When he was to return I considered trying to conceive a child for him. But you are not wrong. It was strangely a blessing that he passed when he did."

We arrived at our destination and quit the carriage. Mother clutched my arm as we walked with the others to the gravesite. She quivered behind her veil as the minister prayed, attempting to squelch her sorrow. I felt my own tears rising in a flurry in compassion for her, and I watched as the Madam wept before the casket, a woman holding to her as it was lowered into the ground. When the flowers had been dropped onto the casket, the funeral party dispersed. Mother became nervous.

"Kate, I think someone has recognized me. We should go back to the carriage at once." We separated from the crowd and returned to the carriage. It seemed a long time until the burial the procession again made movement back to the road. Just before we were to move forward Mother opened the door.

"I'm tired, Kate, tired of this whole situation. I will tell the driver to take us to Longhurst. I cannot live another eighteen years without confronting Alistair."

"But what if he is here at the funeral?"

She shook her head. "No, I did not see him. We will go."

As the other carriages made a right turn at the main road, our carriage turned in the opposite direction. I tried to focus my attention on the countryside as we went. We were delivered to Longhurst's door far more quickly than I could prepare myself.

My heart was palpitating crazily. I allowed Mother to go to the door alone, but as I looked upon her delicate frame, dwarfed before the grand entryway, I knew I must support her, and I hurried to her side. We stood together as she used the enormous brass knocker.

Moments later a butler opened to us. "Yes? State your business."

"We've come to meet with Lord Percy, sir," Mother said.

"Elder, or younger Lord Percy? Elder Lord Percy is away, though I don't suppose either was expecting you," he said, studying us with misgiving.

Mother smiled faintly. "No, sir, we did not give advance warning. Younger Lord Percy would be fine."

"And whom shall I report is calling?"

"Tell him it is Victoria. He will know." The butler ushered us in and closed the door behind us before walking briskly to the east. We grasped hands. When we heard two sets of footsteps approaching, our hearts skipped a beat. Suddenly standing before us were the butler and a sandy-haired young man who appeared to be no older than myself.

"Oh, I *am* sorry! Surely this is confusing for us all! I meant to speak with *Alistair* Percy."

"I asked whether you wished to speak with the elder Percy, madam; you replied that the younger would do," the butler said.

Mother looked bewildered. "You see, I had assumed that by elder you were referring to Lord Franklin Percy."

The young man spoke. "My grandfather has been deceased two years, madam. May I ask what business you have with my father? He is away this morn at a burial, though I wonder if he's made it, as he had a late start."

Mother shook her head. "You mean he is at the burial of Lord Braithwaite?"

"I believe so, madam. I would have attended myself, but I have just returned from a journey abroad. He may not return until evening."

"Forgive me, gentlemen. This has all been overwhelming. I haven't been to Somerset for quite some time, and I have not spoken with Lord Percy for many years. We'd best be going now. By the way, your mother, I've forgotten her name. Is she well?"

"Marcella Lawton? My mother passed of cholera when I was small. Did you know her?"

"Yes, yes I knew her. I'm sorry to hear it. Your mother was a decent woman." He bowed his head in thanks. We turned to leave.

"Madam," said the butler. "What shall we tell Lord Percy?"

"I shall leave my message with him personally."

THE CARRIAGE RIDE BACK to Holmsbridge was an anxious one. The revelation was obvious—Mother was sold so that she may be replaced with another woman, a woman she knew; a woman that may have been pregnant at the same time as her. Mother's countenance was gray. I wanted to ask her questions, but I knew she needed the time to brood, to decide on what she should do next.

When we'd reached Holmsbridge and had been helped from the carriage, I promptly escorted Mother to the Blue Room to lie down.

"All the years I've tried to forget have chased me down, Kate. She ought to have told me Alistair was attending. What if I would have encountered him? I will hide away for the remainder of the evening, but you! Nobody would notice you. You will put on my dress. I will tell you his features and you will pass on my message. Or, if you haven't the heart, you may tell a servant to give it to him."

I did not know how to respond to this. I did not need to. I would do it for her. When I'd donned her mourning gown and we'd elegantly arranged my hair, I emerged from the room a new person. I felt for the first time like a woman. Yes, I could do anything with this kind of confidence.

I walked to the stairwell with the message concealed in my palm. I peered down at the gathering. Such a sea of morbidity! I felt secure enough to join them, as they all seemed too preoccupied to notice me, and I made it down the stairs without acknowledgment. The easy atmosphere surrounding the buffet table was where I felt most comfortable. Neither did I need invitation to reach for a few morsels. As I picked at the tray of bon bons, I searched the room for the man with the description Mother gave me: tall, dark, debonair. But there were many of these in the room. Blue eyes, cheekbones like my own. The Madam was now standing too near for comfort. I moved away.

Alas, there he was! I could not look away; there was something about him, something that felt it must be him. The debonair man with the brilliant blue eyes surveyed the room cautiously. I wondered if he sensed me there, if he felt trapped under my gaze. Had he caught wind that mother was in town? Boldness came to me and fostered my footsteps. I drew nearer.

As if he was prompted by footsteps, he turned and walked away. He appeared to be headed for the veranda. I followed discreetly behind. Once at the door to the veranda, I saw no one, so I ventured out. I dared myself to walk near the hedges and turned my head to listen for movement as the blood coursed wildly through my veins. Hearing nothing, I decided to return to the manor.

"Pardon me," I heard. I gasped. I looked up into the face of my father.

He looked at me curiously, smiled. "I apologize for frightening you. I myself thought I was alone." His smile was endearing, yet I detected an underlying craftiness as he lifted a cigarette to his lips. His dark, well-styled moustache stirred above his pursed lips. His hands gracefully struck a match and held the fire to the tip of the cigarette.

My tongue could not be budged. All my newfound boldness had drained from me like lifeblood from a wound. The message in my hand was forgotten. He inhaled, exhaled a cloud of bluish smoke.

I attempted a smile, trying frantically to think of something to utter. From behind me came Mother's voice.

"No man is ever as alone as he seems, Alistair." My father's expression was not unlike mine had been seconds before. I hurried off around the corner to the other side of the hedges, where I watched with fearsome anticipation.

"What's come over you? Have you seen a ghost?" She inched closer. He could not move. The cigarette between his fingers now hung limply as a browned leaf. "Surely you did not think I would dismiss paying my father his respects in death?"

Finally Alistair gathered himself and laughed blithely. He adjusted the cigarette and took a drag. "Victoria," he said as he exhaled and tapped off the ashes.

"Come, let us be merry. We've much to celebrate. Why, our daughter is about to pass her seventeenth birthday. She reminds me so very much of myself at that age. And yet she has lived such a different life. We both have."

My father looked around him. "Was that her just now?" He lifted his head to the sky and laughed. "You are impudent in the extreme! So you have come to collect for the girl, is that it? Though only God knows whose child it really is, what with all your—"

"How dare you! You know whose child it is. I was not the cheat in our home. Money means nothing to me. What I have come to collect is an apology."

"Apology? For what? Marrying the mother of my son and heir so that he may grow up legitimately? A good thing, too; yours was born a girl," he said. At Mother's stupor, he continued. "Don't you know I had our marriage dissolved just as soon as—" he began, finishing the sentence with a flip of his hand. "I had to clear the smoke for Marcella. There wasn't time to take the decent route. And a divorce trial? Dear God, the infamy that would bring to her name and mine! Desertion charges, Victoria, that made the initial proceedings markedly quick. Getting the prize itself under charge of your alleged adultery, however; now that took a bit of wrangling—money in the right pockets, that sort of thing. A pretty penny it was, too." Alistair took another deep drag from his cigarette.

Mother winced. "Please, accept my heartfelt condolences on Marcella's passing," she retorted icily. "And the boy must be what? Seventeen? Such a fine looking lad."

He took a step forward. "Do not come within ten thousand paces of Jonathan!" he warned, thrusting his index finger at Mother.

"I'm afraid I already have. But you needn't worry. I have no violence in me. Come, Alistair, can't you just make it right? I've not come to cause scandal. Now that I know the dirty tidbits, I should think a thorough explanation is the least you could afford me. Could you really have forgotten me after you'd done it? Didn't you wonder of me, of us?"

"One cannot simply spring up after so many years demanding a bloody explanation. The deuce!" Alistair exclaimed, bemused; his lips arranging into a scowl.

"Why ever not? You have had as long to dwell on it, haven't you?" she asked.

"Perhaps; if one had dwelt much upon the subject." He blinked, flicked his cigarette.

"You considered me dead! That is why you would not have expected to encounter me here today. You thought I had died or that I wouldn't have the courage to show my face again. You underestimate me!" Mother accused, her eyes wide with outrage.

"Scheming snake! I should have seen to your demise personally."

"Oh, Alistair, I think you have done quite enough. You have no idea the hell I have endured at your expense!"

Alistair Percy was not about to be trumped. "You mind who it is you accuse! If you *dare* attempt to pin me to this there will be real hell to pay. No one will believe the words of a cowardly adulteress." He threw his cigarette to the ground and mashed it with the ball of his foot and walked away.

I ran to Mother's aid, for she appeared she would faint. After escorting her to our room, I helped her onto the bed, where she lay limp as a ragdoll

The blackguard! I hated Alistair Percy.

Chapter Six

I left Mother alone in her grief. It was what she requested. If not I would not have left her side, as I feared for her state of mind. I told her I would fetch her a glass of cool water. I knew I should ask a servant to fetch it for me—that was the proper way of doing things—but I could find no one to assist me. They must have all been employed with the gathering. I decided to try to find the stairs leading below to the kitchen.

This was not so simple. How many back staircases could one manor hold? Somewhere in my search, I stumbled upon a cozy library and stepped inside. From there I could hear the soft noises emanating from the party, and somehow it gave the library a clandestine feel that I found irresistible. I fingered some of the hundreds of books on the shelves.

The fortune in those books alone! I wondered how many of them had been read. I pulled one out and sat myself down in a tufted leather chair on the other side of a nearby secretary's desk. It was a book about Egypt. After scanning the pages, I read nothing to interest me and I laid it down on the desk before me. As I did this I noticed a slip of paper sitting upon a stack of thin booklets. It was a letter.

It was not in my nature to spy or eavesdrop. If I had not seen the word "Victoria" just there on the page I would not have read on. The letter was dated nearly two years earlier.

Dearest Master Braithwaite,

After many years of faithful servant-hood to you and yours in the office of governess, I lay on my deathbed with knowledge I feel pressed to expose. For some time I have known the whereabouts of your daughter, Victoria. After the incident, she penned me with her version of the happenings, requesting that I keep it silent. Perhaps she found in my office a sense of refuge.

At the time of the writing she resided in Hazel Grove at Northampton. She has stated that she did not leave Mr. Percy for another man, and has never been to Australia, as he has claimed. I implore you to use this information for the good of the family, to unite and not divide.

Your humble servant, Anastasia

I had assumed Mother at least made an effort to contact my grandparents through the years. Out of the corner of my eye I saw a servant pass with a lantern in hand. It was growing dark and she must be lighting the corridors. I left the room in search of this servant, and finding her at the end of the hall I arrested her. As I was requesting that she deliver Mother a glass of water, another lady came upon us. It was the Madam. My stomach dropped.

"What is the meaning of this?" she demanded after realizing it was I. I tried to deflect her attention from my gown by keeping with my current activity. I bowed and gave a curtsy.

"Mother has asked me to fetch her a glass of cool water. She is not feeling well. I could not find anyone to assist until just now." The Madam eyed the servant.

"Very well, you may go," she said to her.

She turned her back to me, walked along the corridor. I hurried to match her pace.

"What is it our dear Victoria is suffering from, hmm? A bout of nerves?" I pondered whether or not to reveal the nature of Mother's malaise. I dared myself.

"You could say that she has had an encounter with a ghost from the past. 'Twas quite the unpleasant experience, I assure you."

The Madam paused before going on. "Walk with me. We shall have a chat."

I knew this could not be an affirmative experience, though I did not see how to avoid it, as it is rude to decline one's elder and hostess. I walked.

46

"Tell me about your home," she began. I considered being sly with her, but thought better of it.

"There is nothing much to tell, Madam. We live in a hamlet of Northampton where we are caretakers of a farm."

"A farm!" she exclaimed. "And where is your father?"

"I assume you are referring to Earnest, the man who raised me. He died in the War when I was small."

"Ah, a military man then," she said with a level of approval. I did not inform her that his service was forced at Mr. Boyle's hand so that he could brag to his friends of his contribution to the Crown. Let her think he'd been an officer. She continued. "And if he was not your father, how did this Earnest become a part of your life?"

I cleared my throat. "I am not sure that it is my place to respond. I have just learnt a good portion of it myself, including my heritage. From what Mother told me, when the auctioning was taking place, Earnest happened by and took pity on her. He offered a good sum in the bid out of a portion of his master's money that he was to put to the exchangers in London.

"Afterwards he didn't know what else to do with her, so he took her home to live with him. It was quite a sacrifice for him. His master, Mr. Boyle, had been considering promoting him from foreman to a business liaison, but after Mother was brought along, he was left to his original station. It is a marvel he was not let go altogether."

"I see. Well, you're quite well spoken for someone of your—upbringing." The Madam unconsciously brushed off her shoulder as she said this. "Pray, why do you suppose your mother has found it necessary to keep this information from you all these years?"

I bristled. "I gather she did not wish me to think of the life of privilege I could have had. It is difficult enough to keep our spirits up in our condition without grasping for the unreachable."

"Do not play on my sympathies, girl."

"Your sympathies?" I asked.

"One cannot ignore that sympathy is what your mother desires. She always *did* pine for attention. Alistair Percy is a decent, honourable man. He was nothing but proper to your mother. Does she expect me to compensate her poor choices in life with material rewards?"

"For compensation she did not come, but to pay respects to her father. Neither was it my mother's choice to live as a pauper. How foolish the notion! As for Alistair Percy, you may wish to hear her out. From her account their marriage was a cold nightmare. You might give explanation as to why you have not sought contact with your daughter these years." I was treading on dangerous ground speaking to her so.

The Madam stopped cold. "It is not the place of a sniveling child to know such business. Your mother is a fallen woman! Such a woman is dishonourable. Whether or not what she says of Alistair is truth is yet to be confirmed. For all we knew she was dead."

"But you did know. You *knew* she was alive, and further where. And a fallen woman would not live in celibacy as Mother has all these years. I take great offense that you would refer to her as an adulteress."

The Madam stared at me, her lips tightly pursed together.

"Mother would have been much obliged to have been informed that her oppressor was on site this day. If you will excuse me, I must go and help her to pick up the pieces of her shattered ego at the hands of that wretched man. Forgive me, madam." I walked off in a fury.

"Horrible woman!" I cried when I was in the Blue Room.

Mother sat up in bed. "Who? What horrible woman?"

"Your mother! She is awfully cold. Why did you bring me here?"

"Kate, dear, it is you who insisted on coming. Now what is the matter?" I related to her what had just transpired in the corridor. "Oh, dear! You should not have gotten involved. It is all in enough of an uproar."

"But she accused you, and me! And why did you not write to them all this time?"

49

"What do you mean? I have written, once in the beginning, and once again about two years ago. I did not include much of any information but I did wish them to know I was alive."

"That is not what she said! She said she did not know where you were, that you may have been dead for all they knew. And I saw, in the study—I saw a letter from your former governess. She told them where you were just before she died, two years ago."

"Anastasia passed? Oh, I wish I would have known it! Your grandmother does not want the scandal on her hands, and that is her choice. I told her the truth, and how she employs it is none of our business; we have no need of being caught up in this horrid web. We shall live our lives and she shall live hers."

"But Mother! You're just going to let her get away, let *them* get away with this? Do you know that Alistair said you went off to Australia with some man!"

"We will be civil, Kate. Anger will only eat us from within like some wretched disease. It is in our hands to decide our fate now. You will write your grandmother a letter of apology for your brashness, and for getting involved in something you had no right to get involved in."

I made no reply in my stubbornness, yet in the morning I reluctantly penned an apology for my outburst. It was, after all, the right thing to do. Besides, Mother would be angry with me if I hadn't, and I was in no mood for the reprimand.

In the morning I filled my pockets with whatever food had been left uneaten on our breakfast tray and looked around the Blue Room with a sense of regret. We walked down to the foyer and said our goodbyes to the Madam, who stood as erect as ever.

Mother had but a brief conversation with her before we were ushered into the carriage that would take us to Glastonbury Station. As we wheeled along I watched Holmsbridge pass from view. I wondered if I would ever live to visit it again.

Chapter Seven

It was with great emotional effort that Mother and I rounded the bend toward the farm, our footsteps weary and slow. At dusk we came upon it, and from a distance we scanned its landscape. There sat Joseph's cottage to the left nearby the stables, while our cottage was to the right edge of the property near the hen house and smoke house, still partially concealed by trees from our view.

Between our cottages and set further ahead was Chatworthy House. It was a country house, lined on either side with hedges, most assuredly to hide our cottages and the other farm buildings from view. Chatworthy House had long before been Mr. Boyle's primary residence, where he had lived with his wife and their infant daughter, Trudy.

Earnest had been the farm's foreman, and he was in charge of its labour force during growing season, this until he was sent off to fight in the Crimean War when I was three years of age. Mother served as milkmaid for the Boyles, though she did much more in keeping the family gardens and hen house, and a myriad of other details as they came up. The head housemaid and the cook were permitted to keep a room in Chatworthy House. It was the tiniest of rooms just under the eaves, but it was shelter. Another maid, who stayed up the road with her family, took on the laundry as well as the scullery.

Though a governess had been hired to care for Trudy, I was often called upon to help with such duties, though I was small myself and probably in need of just such care, and the other servants used me in numerous ways of service 'round the house. I was frightened of them all, as they treated me brashly.

When Earnest did not return from war, Mr. Boyle permitted us to live as we were, though without the extra income Earnest would have provided us. Subsequently, Mr. Boyle began to employ a transient labourer as foreman each year for the growing season, and he thought it useful to have us on the property in addition to Joseph to keep watch of the goings on. This was a miracle of God, seeing as how when Mother first arrived Mr. Boyle took little liking to her, suspecting that she'd conned Earnest into marriage to escape who knows what sort of fate; perhaps even prostitution.

When Trudy was barely two, and I no older than five, she and her mother fell victim to cholera quite suddenly; this in the late fifties during England's devastating cholera epidemic. After a couple of weeks they both passed on the same day. Shortly after, the governess as well contracted the disease and passed on. All this transpired while Mr. Boyle had been away on business, and he had been unable to return in time to say goodbye. In his grief he ordered us to seal up Chatworthy House and he purchased an estate nearer to town.

Presently, save the cellar kitchen which we would need for our own use, and which had a separate entrance, we sealed up the entire home. This had been the state of Chatworthy House ever since.

Our duties were now to milking the cows, making cheese, butter and jam, growing and canning vegetables, collecting eggs, and other such care-taking chores. Though we partook of our labours, much of the fruits of our labour were either delivered to Mr. Boyle, for use at his estate, or taken to market. Selling the goods was an effort to supplement our measly income, but Mr. Boyle still took a sizable cut of the profits. Nevertheless, in all of it, we were mainly left alone in our daily lives, and that was a blessing in its own rite.

This is why, when at last we came upon our cottage, we were overcome with a shock. There against the jeweled backdrop of dusk, we witnessed a corkscrew of smoke rising from the chimney. Once past the brush, we were able to confirm that someone was indeed within by the orange glow at the windows.

"What do you suppose this is about?" I asked. Mother signaled to me to hush and inched closer to the window.

"It's a strange man!" she whispered. "A gentleman! We must consult Joseph. Surely he will know." We dropped our bags behind a bush and scurried off to Joseph's cottage.

Mother knocked heavily at his door. "Whaddya want?" he shouted from within.

"Joseph! It's Victoria. There is a strange man inhabiting our cottage! Do tell us what this is about. Have we been evicted?"

Joseph grunted. "Ask 'em yerself if you will! What've I to do wiv it?"

Mother turned the doorknob, knowing full well Joseph would be too lazy to open the door for himself.

"I won't carry on a conversation through the door!" There sat Joseph at his hand-hewn table smoking his pipe, the bulbous nose on his weathered face practically casting its own shadow in the firelight.

"Have ye bit yer noses?" he asked with a mischievous smile, exposing dark gaps where his teeth had rotted out. I dared surmise he was glad to see us. Then he soured his face again, as if to remind himself that happiness was not a part of his make-up.

"What will you have, dastardly females!" I'll tell yer anything to get y'outta here."

"The man in our cottage, Joseph—who is he?" Mother was accustomed to his games. Another grunt came out of the old man. At last he conceded.

"The master's 'ired out Chatworthy 'ouse to 'em for the summer. It bein' closed up I tol' 'em to take the cottage till ye come back to make it ready. Now will ye leave me? I won't be disturbed."

"Disturbed? Oh, Joseph! 'Tis you who have disturbed *us*. Why could you not board the man yourself?" Then, looking about Mother concluded the matter on her own, supposing no guest would be comfortable in such a rat's nest.

So much for a man's protection. We left Joseph and went straightaway to the cottage to introduce ourselves.

"Mother, suppose he gives false pretense? Mr. Boyle has never hired out Chatworthy House! And I have no desire to go prowling about within it. I fancy the place haunted."

"Let this stranger see no fear in your eyes. If there is trouble, lunge for the gun on the mantel," Mother instructed

"Lunge for the gun?" I whispered, pushing Mother ahead of me at the cottage door. She raised her hand hesitantly and knocked.

After a moment a gentleman with dark locks pulled open the door. The man smiled an uncharacteristically English smile—a warm smile. My fear dissipated. There would be no need for the gun at the mantel.

I studied him with wide eyes as my cheeks flushed. By his dress and manner he was obviously a part of the gentry, a true gentleman—and our superior. He had a proper English countenance; his features were not particularly noteworthy. His age I placed somewhere between mid twenties and thirty years. He had well-groomed sideburns like any other fellow, in stature was commonly tall and thin; yet his eyes stood apart. Behind them, even at first glance, I saw what sort of immeasurable soul resided there.

"G-good evening, sir," Mother began. I could hear relief in her voice.

"Ah, yes. You must be Mrs. Thurgood, and this is your daughter, I assume," he said, and bowed. When he looked upon me, I turned my eyes downward. We curtseyed in return.

"Yes, I am Mrs. Thurgood, and this is Kate. We regret we were unavailable to welcome you. We have been away on family business and were not aware that Chatworthy House was to be hired."

"Do not trouble yourselves. I myself was not expecting to arrive so prematurely. My original arrangements were to come in a fortnight's time, and to have given plenty of notice. Silly me, I've left you standing in the doorway of your own home. Please, come in." We followed him in. "I only hope you are not offended that I have passed the night here. That kind sir, Joseph, informed me I could stay here until Chatworthy House is made ready."

Kind sir? Joseph?

"Not at all Mr.—how shall we address you, sir?" Mother asked.

"Mr. Roeing, if you please."

"Mr. Roeing, we only hope you have found it adequately comfortable." I was ashamed that a man of his station had spent the night in our cottage, both because it was meager and because it seemed an invasion of our privacy. He had slept in our bunk and used our washstand, and the soap upon it. Why had he not stayed in a boarding house in town? I was suddenly embarrassed by our dirt floor. I supposed he was accustomed to wooden planks. Or better. Marble, perhaps?

"Comfortable, yes," he confirmed. "I hope you don't mind, I have no intention of overstepping my boundaries, but as I lay on the bunk this past night I felt a draft of cold air seeping through some cracks in the wall, so I took care to patch them up today, having nothing pressing to occupy my time. And I daresay the roof will soon be in need of a solid re-thatching, else the elements be on your heads!"

Mother and I glanced at one another, dumbstruck. Our bewilderment did not go unnoticed by our guest.

"Have I offended you?" he asked, his brow furrowed.

"Why no, certainly not! We are merely very grateful for your assistance, though we cannot imagine why you should bother to lend it. Well, you must be very hungry indeed! Permit us to fix you a meal, sir."

Mr. Roeing nodded. "A meal would be very much appreciated, thank you, Mrs. Thurgood. With all respect, are you in mourning?"

We looked down on our black garments. Pity I would be required to wear them six months more, and Mother a few more than that. Those were the rules of etiquette; though I didn't foresee that anyone would have known the difference, cut off from society as we were.

"Sir, yes we are. We are grieving the death of my father. We have only just come from his funeral," Mother answered.

"I offer you every condolence." Mr. Roeing said as he bowed.

"Thank you, sir," Mother answered, her eyes misty. We set off around the hedges for the cellar kitchen at Chatworthy House to prepare the meal.

There wasn't much to come by in the way of ingredients, but Mother thought mutton pie would do well, and we had some plum preserves to serve alongside. She instructed me to fetch some eggs from the hen house and more kindling for the stove.

On my way, I was intercepted by Mr. Roeing. I immediately stood at attention like a member of the Royal Army.

"Please, allow me to accompany you, Kate," he said with a friendly smile. A shiver vibrated down my spine as he said my name.

Not wishing to offend, I curtseyed to imply that he may accompany me. The crackling of the leaves beneath our feet was the only sound for several paces, save the beating of my heart, which I could hear thumping away in my ears.

"Your mother is a quite amiable," Mr. Roeing remarked. I nodded. "Have you a father or do you and your mother abide here alone?" I found the question intrusive. Other servants may have been accustomed to random questioning, but not I.

"My father passed when I was a girl. And Joseph is here."

"Please, I offer my condolences yet again. I only ask in concern for your safety."

"We have a gun, sir."

"I see," he said. "Well, here we are." He awaited me while I gathered the eggs from the hen house.

"I must also gather some kindling, sir," I said when I had re-emerged. I imagined I must be covered in feathers and smelling of dung. I felt my hair for traces of either.

"Permit me to gather the kindling. That basket looks far more becoming in your arms than mine," he said. I blushed.

"Forgive me if I offend you in asking, but is it your custom to assist the servants?" I asked. Most gentlemen would not have given a second glance, much less a kind one, to a servant, especially a female servant; unless he had poor intentions.

He laughed. "I try not to become tangled up in social expectations, if that is what you are implying. I do not wish for you or your mother to be invisible to me, as is the custom in other households. In any case, I am a farm foreman as far as you know, so such delicacies need not be followed strictly here in the country," he said with a wink.

How peculiar.

At dinner I studied this Mr. Roeing, at first fearing he would be put off by the chips in our unmatched dinnerware. He did not seem to notice. Perhaps he was being disingenuous with us now; I could not imagine that anyone was that good in the end. He even offered to sleep in the stables so that Mother and I might feel more comfortable.

I could not wait until Chatworthy House was readied so that he might be a safe distance away.

Chapter Eight

At dawn, Mother and I arose to ready breakfast. After all, we would need a good start to the day if we were to begin the gargantuan task of making Chatworthy House inhabitable again. I set out to the barn to fetch a pail of milk.

I cherished the early morning with its fresh air and pale sunlight. As I stood considering the beauty of the surrounding landscape, I suddenly turned my head to find that I was not alone, and let out a yelp.

"Good morning, Kate," Mr. Roeing greeted. Then he laughed at my surprise, as did Joseph, who standing beside him.

"Skittish are we?" Joseph teased. I frowned at the remark. I noticed that each of them held a container filled with freshly caught fish.

"What are those?" I asked.

Joseph rolled his eyes. He pointed to the fish. "'ese are what the common folk call fish." I noticed that he'd taken care to trim his usually scruffy white beard. Mr. Roeing was having a positive effect on him, to be sure.

"I thought fresh kippers would do well for breakfast, so I asked Joseph to join me in catching some," Mr. Roeing said. Joseph puffed up at the mention of his own name.

"Sir, I apologize. If we had known you desired kippers we would have risen earlier to catch some!"

"Don't be ridiculous. Joseph and I enjoyed the sport. Tell your mother we will have them cleaned for her in mere moments," he said as they disappeared 'round the hedges to the little shack Joseph had built for just this purpose.

I fetched my pail of milk and ran to tell Mother. The kippers made an excellent addition to our skillet cakes and eggs. Joseph joined us for breakfast at Mr. Roeing's invitation, which at first annoyed me, but as Joseph enthusiastically played to Mr. Roeing with interesting tidbits of information, I found myself amused.

"Mrs. Thurgood, allow me to help you unseal the doors at Chatworthy House this morning. I imagine after all these years they will be difficult to pry," Mr. Roeing offered. Joseph cleared his throat.

"Oh yes, 'twould be good to give the girls a proper start," Joseph piped in his best English. Mother and I exchanged doubtful glances at his newfound willingness to help.

"I assume Mr. Boyle has given you some history on the place, sir?" Mother asked our guest.

"I know a little, yes."

"Did he elaborate on the circumstances?" she asked.

"Yes, very tragic indeed," Mr. Roeing said.

"Mr. Roeing, if you please, how is it that you have come to be here to let out Chatworthy House?" I asked. I was surprised at my own forwardness in questioning my superior. Mother glanced at me in warning. Nevertheless, Mr. Roeing gave his answer.

"When in London, I inquired about any place I could hire for the summer where I could act as a foreman to a farm. This amused Mr. Boyle greatly and, as if to bet I could not handle the job, he offered me Chatworthy House. It will be quite a story for him to tell of me if I should fall short, and I surmise there are bets to be won in the process. Besides, he was squarely intoxicated," he whispered as though there were others around to hear him that should not be privy to such information.

Mr. Boyle was indeed a gambler, but the notion was strange. Gentlemen did not generally take over the positions of farm labourers. This would be an interesting summer, indeed.

Mr. Roeing pried open the doors and some windows in Chatworthy House and set off to town to speak with Mr. Boyle, who by now should have returned from London. Mother urged him not to mention that he had stayed in the cottage or the stables, as Mr. Boyle might find the idea reprehensible. Mr. Roeing agreed not to say. Really she did not want it discovered that we had been out of town.

Mother and I took our first steps into Chatworthy House with care. It seemed improper to be there, as though we were trespassing on a gravesite. But there we stood in the dining room. It was as though we stepped into a time warp. The air was dense and gritty, so despite the chill we kept the window open to freshen the air. I immediately set about opening the flue on the fireplace to ready it. There were webs hanging from every corner; no doubt Joseph would have his work ahead in ridding the place of pests.

We uncovered the table and chairs and took the coverings outside. Now the room resembled the way it had been—then.

The memories flooded us. Sweet Trudy struggling to stand, and Mr. Boyle with a hint of good humour on his face, brought to bear by the missus. The paintings on the wall we remembered clearly, and the china in the cabinet, though thickly covered in dust, was just as it had been.

Suddenly it felt like Christmas time, like opening presents. We ran through the house, uncovering furniture at a mad pace. The great measures of dust swirling 'round gave the impression of magical fairy dust. Fairy dust that induced fits of coughing!

The sofa, the imported rug that had been rolled up and stationed in a corner, the marble mantel piece in the parlour; all was familiar. Before visiting Holmsbridge I had considered Mr. Boyle to be the wealthiest man the world over.

It was a good thing Joseph was assigned to clean out the chimneys. I had no desire to emerge from them a blackened creature. As it was, I would be coming away a dingy brown. Joseph began with the parlour hearth as we set about upstairs to the master suite. Mr. Roeing would need it as quickly as possible. Among other things we would need to take apart the iron bed completely, wiping down each nook with a solution of borax. The layers of bedding constituting the mattresses would need to be taken apart, and their contents sifted and aired. From what it appeared, the mattresses were mainly stuffed with horse hair, and a straw layer, which was missing, would need to be made fresh. Keating's powder would need to be used liberally to stave off bed bugs and other mites. It would be a dozen times worse than a usual spring cleaning with all the years of accumulated grit.

Before we set about this task, we opened the linen cupboard, where lay all the white bed linens, mattress coverings, and blankets of various rich colours, folded neatly as though they had been placed there just a day earlier. Someone had the foresight to place a large number of lavender strands between them to keep away insects. I took what linens were salvageable down to the scullery bin to scrub them and hung them to dry in the warmth of our cottage.

I returned to the room to find Mother chasing away a family of mice that had made their home in a corner. "Child, this is a nightmare!" she said under her breath.

"Let us get everything out of the wardrobe and then we'll take the bed apart," I suggested. "Joseph can carry down the mattresses to be aired and then he can see to all the critters." Really I wanted to pick through Mrs. Boyle's old wardrobe. The clothing was splendid still, even if outdated. Further examination, however, turned up evidence of moth corruption. We would rework what was not damaged into something more modern, being thankful for the gift of quality fabric.

I took one of the petticoats from its hanger and held it against myself in the mirror. Then I donned the matching hat and did my best impression of Mrs. Boyle.

"Dear Mr. Boyle, you haven't the slightest *idea* what you are saying! Why, if the Queen were to make her way through Hazel Grove *this day* her very first station would be here at Chatworthy House! We are, after all, the most important of people!" I threw myself piously upon the bed, causing a cloud of dust to rise up about me like a swarm of gnats.

Mother took up an old pipe and followed suit.

"My dear, dear Mrs. Boyle, I suppose that if the Queen herself were to come to this, our humble abode, you would nary be satisfied until you banished me to the stables to converse with the cattle while you, most exquisite of women, kept Her Majesty all to yourself." She, too, threw herself on the bed and we burst into laughter. At the unexpected sound of applause we shot up.

"Bravo! Encore!" shouted Mr. Roeing. We were sorely embarrassed and began our apologies. Normally if servants were caught speaking or giggling during the work day there was punishment to follow. Mr. Roeing raised his hand to silence us.

"No, no. I should like to thank you for that bit of theatre." He laughed. Was he scorning us? We exchanged puzzled glances. Mother cleared her throat and stood up, smoothing her skirts.

"I trust your visit with Mr. Boyle was promising, sir," she said.

"It was fine, thank you. It was a marvelous morning for a long stroll, and Mr. Boyle was in high spirits."

"Wonderful, sir. Did Mr. Boyle leave you with any instructions as to our duties? Will he or you be hiring on any staff to run Chatworthy House, or are we to suit that office? As it stands we have much to care for in the summer months."

"Oh, well, part of my duties as foreman of the farm this summer will be to oversee the family gardens, as well as chopping the wood. You won't have to worry for that. Mr. Boyle has made a shift regarding your duties, which shall now be to me for as long as I stay. I suppose you could call yourselves maids-of-all-work, though you, Mrs. Thurgood, shall have the distinction of Housekeeper."

"Sir, we shall do our best, though we haven't served in that capacity for many years; I mean to say the domestic capacity. And we've the milking to attend to, and the butter and cooking—we only hope to be adequate for your needs."

"Mrs. Thurgood, all will be well! There will be a hired girl at your disposal to assist with the milking and butter. Perhaps we'll hire another girl for the scullery. And I? If you are asking for orders, I rarely take to giving them. Yet for your own directives I suppose my desires are quite simple. I require breakfast in the breakfast room, the midday meal I shall take with the workmen, tea in the parlour, and a light dinner, in the dining room. The house will need its keeping as well—no small task—and my clothing and the linens will need washing."

"Sir, be assured that we will do our best for you. The house will take a few more days at best to finish, and after we shall be able to focus more on our culinary skills. As it is, there is barely enough to offer for a decent tea service."

Mr. Roeing grasped Mother's shoulders. "Do not worry a trifle for me. Whatever you have to offer for tea will do. In time you will see how easy I am to please. Tomorrow you may purchase supplies for the larder, whatever is lacking, and you may have a weekly credit for such items. But be advised, aside from a quality tea I do not require fancy fare; I enjoy good country food."

"Are you certain, sir? A credit for the larder?" Mother asked in astonishment. Mr. Roeing laughed.

"Dear Mrs. Thurgood! From now on you shall earn fair wages. This afternoon I would be obliged if you would take tea with me, you and Kate, and each day after. It will be a good time to discuss the goings on of the farm."

How strange, this man! Taking tea with his servants! Nevertheless, as our new master, we would oblige him in whatever his request, strange or not. Not that such requests pained me in the least—and our wages were to be triple our former earnings! It was to be the best summer of my life!

Chapter Nine

By May our entire world had changed so favourably I began to wonder if any of it was real. The work was hard but pleasing, and Mr. Roeing dealt with us far more kindly than any master we had encountered or had even heard of. Mother and I were grateful for his companionship that small remainder of spring, and he ours.

Mother and I had been able to rework some of Mrs. Boyle's old clothing into serviceable new outfits, so that we felt more akin to ladies than mere servants. And with our earnings we were able to purchase a few new things to tidy up our cottage—including a wonderful oval rug and a tea pot that had not a single crack.

The growing season was underway and the fields were being worked by the new Hodges, or farm hands. The Hodges found Mr. Roeing as their foreman rather amusing. But Mr. Roeing was amiable, and since this was a rarity among foremen, they allowed him the liberty without making too much fuss.

On Easter we shared dinner together, and Mother helped me make my first ever Simnel cake, a round fruit cake decorated with balls of marzipan. I was proud of my creation, and I beamed like a sunflower when Mr. Roeing praised it. I chased away the notion that we fit together like a real family that day. And I tried not to imagine that Chatworthy House was mine, though it was difficult.

Following dinner, Mr. Roeing requested that we stay a while longer and play the piano with him. We knew this was an unjust crossing of the line: this was blatant fraternizing with the servants. Since there was nobody around to tattle on us, we all turned a blind eye.

Mother knew a bit of piano, but much of the knowledge was dull to her after so many years of not playing. And ever since I was given a sound paddling as a girl after being caught fingering the keys, I had been afraid to so much as set foot in the near vicinity of a piano.

Mother gave the keys a tickle and slowly reacquainted herself with them. Soon she was playing a long forgotten song. I hadn't realized what a fine singing voice she had.

Next, Mr. Roeing took a turn. A master he was at it, and his singing was mesmerizing. I, for one, was transfixed. All too suddenly he stopped. I opened my eyes to find his eyes upon me.

"Sir?" I asked.

"It is your turn, Kate," he said. Protesting vehemently I was nonetheless ushered to the piano bench and given my first lesson. At the start all was confusing, but at my first successful keying of a child's nursery song, I was enraptured with the art of playing. I would come to spend many stolen moments practicing at that piano while everyone was away at their duties.

It was during one of these stolen moments that I was interrupted by Mr. Roeing. My fingers slipped in my surprise, making for a cacophony of sour notes. I winced, hoping this did not aggravate him.

"I've been meaning to address something with you, Kate." I quickly closed the piano keys and stood to hear his matter, which must of course be that I needed to stop playing when I ought to be working.

"There is one room in the upper level that has yet to be opened." I breathed with relief, although this topic was no more pleasant.

"Yes, sir, that was the nursery; Trudy's nursery."

"I am more than aware that making Chatworthy House inhabitable once again has been an undertaking of extreme proportions, and that your work keeps you quite occupied. But for what reason have you neglected this chamber?"

"Perhaps it's the memories, sir. Besides, I did not think you would have cared to have a readied nursery."

"I would have it opened just the same. The upper floor could benefit from a cross breeze through the corridor. And consequently I may be entertaining guests soon. Surely you understand." He looked firmly into my eyes and walked away.

There it was. It was in my charge to do the unthinkable. I trudged upstairs, stopping short of the nursery door. No, I was not yet prepared for that. I must first train my mind. I wandered into a guest bedroom and studied myself in the vanity mirror.

At the sight of my plain complexion (not rosy as some of the other girls my age,) and the drabness of my hair, severely pulled back and pinned as a chicken's wings before it is to be boiled, I shuddered and focused instead on the contents of one of the drawers. How had I missed it? There lay a shapely bottle of perfume, adorned with a purple silk ribbon. It was the very picture of femininity. The label read, *"Au Cour, eau de parfum."*

I could not imagine what those words meant. Though the vessel had long been emptied, the scent remained. It smelled of roses, and dew. I pretended to dab some behind each ear as I had seen Mrs. Boyle once do. I wondered if it would be considered theft if I lifted an object no person cared for. Its contents were empty, after all. I decided not to take a chance and I slipped it back into the drawer. It was time to carry out my duty.

Knowing Mr. Roeing would soon be up to inspect my work, I forced myself to open the door, if only a crack. It was dark, and the smell of mildew permeated the air. I rushed to uncover the window. In a flurry of dust, I slowly turned and examined the room. Many of Trudy's belongings were in plain sight: a basket of toys, her blankets stacked at the foot of the crib, her toy pram. Suddenly a memory flashed before my eyes, one I would have chosen to keep in the recesses of my mind forever.

I opened the window to let in fresh air and walked shakily from the room, closing the door behind me. I would come back later—the room needed airing or I would choke, I told myself. Before descending the stairs I composed myself. At the foot of the steps Mr. Roeing sat in the drawing room reading over some papers. I was unlucky to have been spied.

"Is everything all right?" he asked. "You don't look well."

I hated being probed.

"The room will need to air out. And it is time to help Mother in the kitchen just now," I fumbled.

"As you see fit. I will see you at dinner." Lately we'd been sharing the evening meal with Mr. Roeing in addition to tea.

I nodded before running off to the cottage. To avoid any more questions, I feigned illness for dinner that night, which could hardly be classified as feigning. Due to my nerves I was perspiring and suffering stomach cramps. The following morning I coyly persuaded Mother to finish in the nursery while I prepared breakfast. By that evening I would have run out of excuses. Mr. Roeing convinced Mother that I could use a private piano lesson after dinner.

"Vivaldi," he said in explanation. I bristled at the thought of being there alone with him, and I was sure he knew it.

After a short music lesson, Mr. Roeing walked in the direction of the fireplace.

"That will be enough for now. Won't you join me here by the hearth?" He motioned that I sit in one of the winged back chairs. I made my way over to the chair and sat down. I assumed he was trustworthy; nevertheless I couldn't be sure. He paced for a bit before sitting opposite me.

"Kate, I did not invite you here tonight for a piano lesson alone. I wish to speak with you in private. You see, I have been studying you these past weeks, taking note of your mannerisms, getting a sense of your character. You are really a very lovely soul; quite delicate and pure. This is so rare. In fact I cannot recall meeting another like you." I shifted in my chair, my eyes downcast.

"You're far more intelligent than others of your status. However, even at this moment you are exhibiting an unnatural fear toward me. You are very nearly trembling. Why? Why do you experience this fear? I want to understand it. Is there something I have done to cause this?" His tone was so very tender. I could not answer him.

"I mean you no harm whatsoever, of that you are assured. I only wish that you could feel at ease with me." He checked the time on his pocket watch absentmindedly.

At last I found my tongue. "I do apologize, Mr. Roeing! You have been so wonderful to us, and nothing if not kind and generous. I do not wish to offend you or repay you with evil. Please, I ask your forgiveness if I have done either."

"You see! There it is again!" he exclaimed. His eyes lit up with curiosity. He rose from his chair and began pacing. "I only wish to understand it. And yet I believe I hold the key to this mystery. Permit me to ask, why does the nursery frighten you so? Why can you not bear to set foot in it?"

I began to grow resentful of all the questions. Why should I bare my soul to him? Why should he know anything? And why had he been peeping at me? I hardened my countenance.

"I do wish I could explain, sir. Perhaps I'm frightened of ghosts." Mr. Roeing bent down and clasped my hand. I drew it back impulsively. He rose again and walked from me. He tossed his pocket watch, then caught it. His eyes were set on a painting on the wall.

"What happened to you there, Kate? In the nursery? Someone, some man, did something to you there. Why else would every male in your world seem a threat?"

I gasped and turned to face him, my expression full of wonderment and pain. He turned his face to me as well. I saw angst there in his eyes, and I turned away once again.

"I have to go now," I whispered. Getting to my feet proved a task in itself. He came near, stood before me. His gaze was fatherly.

"Who was it, Kate? Who did this to you?" His compassion for me, his understanding of my unspoken shame caused my tears to overrun like a swollen embankment.

It had been Mr. Boyle that had done something awful to me in that nursery. Not only had I never spoken it, I had tried with all that was in me to forget it. How could he have known? How could anyone be aware of such a thing at all? Was I not the only soul to have endured such a hell? I didn't know it then, but this sort of thing was a common horror among the servant class.

Mr. Roeing handed me his handkerchief and stood by as I wept for some time. When at last I found the courage to lift my puffy face, I found him looking at me with benevolence.

"I would never lift a finger against you, Kate, you must know that. As long as I am near I won't allow anyone to harm you. That is my word."

I believed him.

Chapter Ten

It seemed we had been sitting in our pews for hours by the time the vicar brought the service to a close. Tonight would be, after all, the night of the Midsummer bonfire, and the entire town was erupting with anticipation. There were games awaiting our play and music to hear and food to pass 'round, and only the remainder of the day to fit it all in.

Mother and I took in the sight as we stepped out of the chapel. Throngs, or what I had considered then to be throngs before ever I had the experience of London, were bustling about. There was a sudden influx of new housing there in Hazel Grove, causing a good bit of crowding on the main avenue. Rumor was that cottages such as ours were becoming quite popular in the face of the crowding and were being purchased by those who could afford to fix them into dreamy idyllic masterpieces, the kind you now find painted on porcelain. We wondered how long we would be permitted to continue to dwell in our own cottage before Mr. Boyle would grow greedy enough to sell it out from beneath us. We would have no recourse in such an event.

As Mother and I walked along, the postmistress, Mrs. Bunting, called after us.

"Oh, Mrs. Thurgood! Yoo-hoo!" We cringed at the familiar voice and turned to face her.

"Darlings, how *are* you?" she said with a deceptively sweet inflection. "Why, it has been ages since last you visited the Post!" It was our custom to visit the Post Office once per quarter, but even then we were not guaranteed to find anything addressed to us. Before the last letter from Holmsbridge, we hadn't received a letter for over a year. There must be something she was seeking after.

She studied us with gluttonous eyes until I began to wonder if we were to be the main course of the day. "There has been a letter tucked aside at the Post until your next visit. I might have sent it along in the mail bag that now goes to Chatworthy House, but Kate, it could be very special indeed!" She held out a small letter between her pudgy fingers. It was addressed to me! My first ever letter!

"Oh, Mrs. Bunting! Thank you so very much!" I cried. I could scarcely repress my desire to tear it open just then and discover its contents. Alas, Mrs. Bunting and her circle of gossips would have to endure, for I would not allow myself to reveal to her a bit of it. I moved the letter behind my back. Her eyes hungrily followed it.

"It was so good of you to deliver it, Mrs. Bunting," I said.

"Yes, well, I wouldn't have wanted you to miss it. It could be very important news. I say, I cannot remember the last time I have come upon a letter addressed in your name. You must be beside yourself with glee!" She wiggled her fingers as she said this. "Do not think me a bother, go ahead! Break the seal! I will help you to read it," Mrs. Bunting urged.

"I—I can't," I stammered. I have already promised myself I would wait until after the bonfire. And Mother can help me read. There is so much excitement presently, and I—I must have a taste of Mrs. Beesley's famous corn cake." I knew my excuse was odd.

"I see," said Mrs. Bunting, her smile falling into a barely obscured grimace of contempt. "Do not neglect to inform us of any exciting news. Good day," she said as politely as she could manage.

She had assumed I could not read. I suppose it was unusual for a girl in my position to have this skill. I had learned the basics from the Sunday school at the rectory for the underprivileged, and lately Mother had been helping me along by borrowing from the library at Chatworthy House, though there was scarcely time to read at all.

The moment we were out of her sight I tore the seal open as a wolf tears into its prey. Mother motioned for me to halt. "Wait. Mr. Roeing is trying to get my attention."

Beside the town's rival church stood Mr. Roeing, waving to Mother. He was surrounded by many of the prominent townspeople, among them the esteemed Mr. Boyle.

"I shall await you here," I said, as I disliked conversing with those haughty people. I hoped Mr. Roeing would be remaining for the festivities; somehow I had imagined we would experience them together. We weren't at Chatworthy House, however, and I could not expect things to go on in public as they did there. I watched Mr. Roeing interact formally with Mother. I found a bench and deposited myself upon it, tapping the letter impatiently on its surface.

"G'day," said a young man with an accented voice as he approached me. I was startled.

"What's the matter, did I scare ya?" he asked. I shook my head timidly. This face was familiar. It was one of the Hodges hired by Mr. Boyle to mind the farm that season. He was a Mick, an Irishman.

"I say, I've seen you 'round the farm, girl." He paused to light up a freshly rolled cigarette. "What's yer name?" he asked with it perched between his lips.

His eyes were as bright and intense as a new coin. Perhaps the attention he was giving me was due to the fact that I was now out of my mourning clothes and into something that brought more colour to my complexion. It was good to be rid of black, especially in the heat of summer. I told the boy my name.

"That's a nice name," he said with a marvelous smile. He sat down casually beside me, leaning back and crossing his leg to rest his ankle on his knee. "My name's Ethan," he said, holding his hand out to shake mine. I shook it weakly, feeling uncomfortable at his touch.

"Pleased to meet you," I croaked. I looked over at Mother, who appeared to be finishing up her business.

"Yep, me an' the others been stayin' up at one of the lodgin' houses fer the summer. Nice enough place," he said, blowing out a thin blue stream of smoke. I noted that his eyes were the colour of moss, and sly. I thought his straight nose to be adorable, and the tufts of dark hair popping out from beneath his cap gave his eyes even more distinction against his pallid, freckled skin.

Mother was now headed in our direction. Ethan must have seen her too.

"Anyway, I guess me friends'll be waitin' on me. Saw ya there and thought I might say 'ello. I guess I'll be seein' ya then,

Kate." He held his hat to his chest, smiling dynamically yet again, and evaporated into the crowd.

"Who was that?" Mother questioned.

"Oh, that was, um, one of the farm hands. He stopped by to say hello." I explained, hoping my face was not glowing red.

"Mr. Roeing informed me that he will be taking refuge with the Bellhouse family tonight and that we needn't worry ourselves with preparing breakfast for him," she said.

The Bellhouse's eldest daughter, Josephine, was quite beautiful. I sulked at the news.

"Well? The letter! Open it!" Mother urged. I had forgotten. I tore it open and read it aloud.

Holmsbridge, 19 June, 1870

Dearest Katherine,

Despite our precarious meeting earlier this year, I have found it in my heart to invite you to Holmsbridge for the holiday season. Already I am wearied of mourning and a little company would do me well. Your Aunt Betina has been staying with me, but it is time to let her return to her own life.

I have invited your cousin Isabella as well, with hopes you will enjoy one another's companionship. Do understand that under the circumstances you would be posing as a friend of hers. If you accept I shall expect to see you mid-November.

Give your mother my regards.

Lady L. Braithwaite

I folded the letter with conflicting emotions. On the one hand I was honoured to have been invited back and to meet a cousin, but how could I leave Mother alone for the holidays? Mr. Roeing had not made it clear how long he would be residing at Chatworthy House. I gave Mother an inquisitive glance.

"Well it isn't my choice! Although I feel if you are inclined to go, you should," she said. I shook my head.

"I would never desert you, Mother! Especially not during the holidays!"

"Tish and nonsense! You're nearly a woman now. You've your own path to follow. People in our position need to be creative. Is this what you want for the rest of your life? To live the way we do? One day I will be gone and if you don't do something now—you must think of yourself now."

"Mother!" We stopped walking as she secured my gaze.

"Kate, God puts opportunities in our path. It is up to us to accept them, and it is nobody's fault but our own if we do not. Think of what kind of opportunity this may be. Your grandmother could be the one to introduce you to a handsome beau, one that could supply you with a wonderful life. Or perhaps she might supply you with education so that you could support yourself as a governess."

"This Isabella could be real trouble. What if it is a trap of some sort?"

"You won't know if you stay here withering away on the farm. If it is a trap you can come home. You are strong, you can handle it." I sighed.

"I will think upon it," I said as I put the letter in my pocket.

Off we trotted to take part in the celebration. This would be the only labour-free day of the year for us, as the maid-of-all-work is not afforded full days of leisure or holiday, only Sunday afternoons. But Mr. Roeing was so kind, so kind to give us the entire day!

We set out to enjoy ourselves to the fullest extent. We ate pulled beef, steamed puddings, and tarts. We played games, watched a spectacle put on by the townspeople, and at last enjoyed a nap beneath a willow tree, our bellies moaning against their load. Dusk was arriving and the townspeople congregated at the town square in preparation for the great bonfire lighting. But first it was customary to choose the Summer Queen from among the young ladies.

The chosen virgin must be beautiful and lively. She would be crowned with a wreath of lilies and paraded around the bonfire on the shoulders of the townsmen. Her prize: a coveted basket of oranges, or at least they were coveted in my eyes.

I had always dreamed of being Summer Queen.

Thus, the minister of the rival church and the town treasurer walked through the gathering of hopeful young candidates and selected a final grouping. Each was sublime in their finest suit of clothes. They peered obligingly at the judges beneath showy hats with plumes and ribbons and gay flowers Was it possible to have this gaiety, or were they performing? I could not imagine being so carefree.

Among the chosen group was Josephine Bellhouse, her raven curls bouncing about in her excitement beneath the brim of her white bonnet with its satin blue ribbon. I let my eyes wander through the crowd after I looked over the girls. Mr. Roeing caught my eye from across the gathering and gestured to me.

I pointed at myself, for I was unsure whether he was communicating with me or another. He smiled again and nodded. Ah, he was urging me to join the group of girls. I shook my head and giggled as if to say, "You are surely crazed."

Still, he persisted. The thought occurred to me that he was making mockery of me. I would not play into it. I allowed those around me to step ahead of me and hid myself behind a large man. From there I heard the announcement of the new Summer Queen, Josephine Bellhouse.

"Good, he can have her," I said under my breath. I clutched Mother's hand and asked if we could leave so that I would not have to witness her being paraded about.

"But dear, they haven't lit the bonfire yet." I knew I had no chance of escaping. I must endure Josephine's parade. I kept my eyes elsewhere as she smiled triumphantly, gushing praises from her perch as she held to her basket of oranges. The townspeople cheered wildly as their new queen graced their presence. As she passed our way, the basket tilted and an orange rolled out, stopping at my feet. I snatched it up and hid it in my skirts before anyone saw.

The townsmen set the enormous piling of brush and wood alive. I stared ahead as the flames shot up into the night, wagging as the tongues of angry wives, thinking of what I had just witnessed with the lily-wreathed Josephine Bellhouse. How the flames were a perfect reflection of my thoughts! The crowd was now a bucket poured to the brim, destined to topple over and spill. Many were already far beyond their limit of gin and ale, and this I knew to mean that the celebrations were waning.

"I trust you ladies are having a splendid evening," Mr. Roeing said, and my attention was returned to the present.

"Sir, indeed we are. And how has your day been spent? With plenty of gaiety we hope," asked Mother. I kept my eyes apart from Mr. Roeing's face.

"I say, yes Mrs. Thurgood." He looked to me. "Kate, did you not see me motioning to you just then?" Mother had not seen this interaction and looked at me in confusion. My eyes darted between the two of them. I smiled and shrugged.

"Forgive me, sir, I'd assumed you were communicating with another," I said. I knew he did not believe me.

"Pity," he answered. "I should have thought you would join the other girls. You might have made a lovely Summer Queen."

I scoffed inwardly. How ridiculous! If there were a girl anywhere in the world with less charm as I, I would have loved to know her.

"Dear, Mr. Roeing!" Mother said as she giggled, "You know Kate is not—"she began, then attempted to salvage her words. "Kate is much too reticent to think herself worthy of the honor."

"Indeed," said Mr. Roeing, "Perhaps next year then," he said as he tipped his hat, "if you are not by then betrothed." I concealed a giggle at the absurdity of his implication. "What is this?" he asked, touching my hand, the one holding to the escaped fruit, now only partially concealed by my skirt.

"It fell. From the basket," I said, suddenly feeling ashamed.

"Do you fancy oranges?" he asked, his eyes probing. I nodded.

"Then I shall be sure to have some ordered. Good evening, ladies." He bowed and walked off. I felt like a child. I didn't want oranges ordered for me—I wished to be elected worthy of them.

"Kate," Mother pointed at me, "Complimentary behavior is part of a gentleman's duty, and one compliment can turn a girl into a right fool. You'll do well to remember that anything offered to you out of duty is likely unmerited."

As the fiddlers began to play their seduction to the crowd and the couples were swept up in dance around the bonfire, I made my mind up to stop entertaining foolish thoughts concerning myself with Mr. Roeing.

Chapter Eleven

I spent the months of July and August busily attending to all my responsibilities, with one extra delight: Ethan, the Mick I had met in town, began speaking with me now and then at the farm. His smile always captivated me, and I hoped I didn't act a fool when he did so. I began to look for him each day, and watch from afar as he worked the fields. Sometimes he whistled a tune as he worked, and I smiled in the moments he would roll up his sleeves to reveal his strong arms, now browning nicely under the late summer sun.

One day in particular as I served the Hodges their afternoon meal, Ethan engaged me in conversation. Looking up, I noticed that Mr. Roeing was looking on from beneath a tree where he'd been having a rest. There was alarm in his eyes. I hoped he was jealous. At the same time I feared he'd scold me for fraternizing during the work day. He got up from his place and walked over, just as Ethan was leaving. I felt my heart skipping erratically.

"Kate," he said, "I have just received a letter from a colleague of mine who is passing through town in two days' time. I thought it best to offer he and his wife the hospitality of a spare room. I would commission you and your mother to prepare a room; also that you stay on to serve a formal dinner that evening. I hope this is no trouble."

That evening would be my seventeenth birthday.

"Not at all, sir," I said with a smile, though I had never served in this manner before and was rattled about learning in such a short frame of time. This was not the sort of birthday wish I would have been inclined to make.

Frantically Mother and I made all ready for Mr. Roeing's guests the day of their arrival. Mother had much to do in training me as a parlour maid. This meant I was to serve the meal, course by course, with precision. Between courses I was to stand by the sideboard, perfectly still as though I were part of the wallpaper. And I would be regarded in much the same manner as a sheet of wallpaper as well.

By six o'clock we heard the carriage approaching. When Mother opened the door for them I swallowed hard. These were people of great pomp.

"Ah, Mr. and Mrs. Dunham! How wonderful to see you again!" Mr. Roeing greeted them after they'd been escorted to the drawing room.

The feathers on Mrs. Dunham's hair ornament were so numerous that, despite her heft, I began to wonder how it was that her feet were still firmly on the ground, for she seemed liable to fly away like a bird soaring on the wind. I considered that it must be the weight of her jeweled brooch holding her earthbound, the largest I had ever seen.

Mr. Dunham was no less posh in his fine suit of clothes, sweating rather like a hog though he was, dabbing now and then at his wetted beard and forehead with a silk handkerchief that bore his initials in fine blue embroidery. He, too, was wearing jewelry, namely a large golden ring with a diamond center and a pocket watch fit for a king, which he proudly displayed on a thick gold chain. Even Mr. Boyle in all his attempts at grandiosity failed to compare.

In the company of the Dunhams was a lady in waiting that looked every bit as snobbish as her employers. She brushed past me without so much as a greeting. Fortunately during dinner she would be eating below stairs and I would not have need of interaction with her.

After I took their headwear and accessories, and Joseph had seen to their other belongings (proudly playing the part of footman), the Dunhams disappeared for a spell to rest and to change for dinner. Mr. Dunham soon came down in a debonair smoking jacket and black tie, followed by Mrs. Dunham in a stylish lavender silk gown and a lacy fan in hand, which she waved dramatically before her face. I feared that in the heat her rolls of flesh would burst out of her corset as a rising round of bread dough.

After hors d'oeuvres and conversation in the parlour, dinner was served promptly at eight o'clock in the dining room. The cooking was all to Mother, and the serving was all to me. I lifted the plates containing the first course, cucumber soup, from the dumb waiter, and nearly walked into the shelf on the wall as I turned the corner into the dining room. Steadying my hands, I breathed and regained my composure before entering the room. My service went smoothly, and in due time I returned with the main course, roast quail with carrots vichy.

"So tell us then, Edward, how *did* you find this quaint little nook?" Mr. Dunham addressed Mr. Roeing. Mr. Dunham's eyes darted about the room with a nostalgic gleam.

Edward!

"Well, I was in London in February and I came across a certain Mr. Boyle, with whom I dined one evening. I learned that he owned this place and I convinced him to let it to me for the season at least. I told him I wished to be a foreman, experience the plight of the labourer first hand. I thought it mightily interesting, don't you?" The Dunhams laughed.

"Why, Mr. Roeing?" Mrs. Dunham paused to give him an exaggerated wink, which of course puzzled me. "Why not one of the manors on the sea? The accommodations are far better, and of course the recreation is incomparable. A foreman! The plight of the labourer! Ha!" said Mrs. Dunham with a great belly laugh. She sounded a swine in my opinion, and if she were I'd soon have her fried up like a side of bacon.

"This was Mr. Boyle's reaction as well," Mr. Roeing said. "That is how I persuaded him to let me stay. As of now there are quite a few bets going that I won't make it to harvest. You know how Mr. Boyle loves his betting—and his liquor. Anyway, this house had been closed up for many years and I wished to stay somewhere, well, old fashioned."

"And how is your little experiment faring?" asked Mr. Dunham. Experiment! As though men's lives were so trite and trivial!

"I should say it is faring quite well. The common folk are wonderfully refreshing." I resented this comment. "And the fresh air has done me wonders to help me think clearly. As you know I have quite the important decision to make come summer next."

"I daresay!" Mrs. Dunham exclaimed. "I can't remember ever a gentleman electing to forego Season. I understand it to be one of the most important decisions of your life, yet to be absent from Season and all its glorious affairs?

However are you to be sure you've found what you are looking for? Or does the gift I brought have anything to do with this?" she asked in a sing-song manner.

Mr. Roeing cleared his throat. He looked up and motioned to me soberly. I knew he meant that I should clear their plates and bring in dessert. I tried not to make mind of the formality between us.

"Ah yes! Season, with all its balls and gentleman's parties and parlours overflowing with gossip! You know I am not in the business of scandal, and my alliances are already quite strong. I should think Society will survive a mere season without me in attendance. As for a decision—

Season? Society? Decision? What did it all mean? The answer I was so hoping to hear would have to wait. At that moment as I was lifting away Mrs. Dunham's plate, it slipped from my fingers and shattered onto the floor. She let out a shriek and lit out of her chair as though all the hounds of Hades were chasing after her.

"Incompetent country girl! Oh, I'm ruined! My nerves have been rustled and I'll not be able to settle them! If I were you, Mr. Roeing—this girl should be flogged—oh!"

Mr. Roeing rushed to her.

"Dear Mrs. Dunham, it is nothing! Let us adjourn to the drawing room. We shall take dessert there. Perhaps you would like to play us a song on the piano. You know how I fancy your playing." Mrs. Dunham glared at me before allowing Mr. Roeing to usher her away.

"I'll tend to dessert," Mother whispered to me as I cleaned up the pieces. She must have heard the commotion from downstairs. When I had reached the refuge of the kitchen, tears began to escape from my eyes.

What would Mr. Roeing think of me now? I realized the Dunham's lady servant was there in the kitchen with me. I read on her face pure insolence, even satisfaction, at my disgrace. She and her lady were a perfect match. I ran upstairs and out the back entrance.

I found refuge in our small flower garden, hidden at the back of our cottage. At this time of year it was alive with colour and lush blooms; my little piece of heaven. I knew the city folk longed to have this pleasure and I appreciated it fully, despite the hardships we endured to have it. I picked a small bouquet of snapdragons, roses, and daisies and continued on to another refuge, the old swing Earnest had strung up for me as a girl on a branch of a giant oak tree.

It was in the perfect location, out of sight of both Chatworthy House and our cottage, and only a stone's throw from the creek. When I was small I spent every moment I could wading in the creek and skipping stones. I walked over and picked some pussy willow to add to my bouquet. I didn't dare wade in the creek past dusk.

The moon magically illuminated the swing. I placed a daisy behind my ear, and a rosebud just above it, tucked securely into my hair. I pretended I was a fairy as I mounted the old relic.

I prayed the swing would remain intact, for I needed it so. I swung, putting my head back and looking up at the great oak tree that supported the swing. It swayed with me, our rhythm one. Silly that it should comfort me after all that time! I began to hum. Tears rolled down my cheeks like drops of warm summer rain.

Dear God, I thought, *I don't belong here. But where? Where do I belong?*

Perhaps Mother had been right. What did I have to fear in going to visit the Madam? Mr. Roeing? He wasn't mine. What future did I have here? Mr. Roeing's guests were what they were. I was what I was. I knew I could not have expected to be treated any differently.

I began to resent Mr. Roeing for introducing the idea that we, as his servants, were worthy of being treated with respect. It was the stuff of fairytales. Now I began to think that if I went to my grandmother there was a small chance that I could be someone else, someone improved. At least I could pretend for a while.

"Kate?"

I started, wiping the tears from my eyes and smoothing my hair and skirts.

"Kate? Are you there?"

I stood. "Y-yes?" I whispered into the darkness. "Mr. Roeing?"

Suddenly he was before me, glowing as magically in the light of the moon as the old swing had. He smiled, and then his countenance changed to one of concern. I was relieved that he was not perturbed with me.

"Are you well, Kate?"

I must have looked horrendous after my crying spell; and I hoped he didn't think me a child for using the swing. He brushed the loose strands of hair back from my face, touched the flowers behind my ear. A faint smile appeared on his lips again. I quivered. I was suddenly intensely aware of my surroundings: the heaviness of the summer air, the crickets playing their song.

"Your mother said I might find you here. Have you been crying?" he asked but did not await my answer. "It was a mere accident. Don't take it to heart."

I looked down. There he went again, offering compassion. I shook my head in confusion.

"All is well, sir. I can only hope Mrs. Dunham's nerves are calmed and that she will rest well. I owe her an apology."

Perhaps he had come to ask me to smooth the bed for her royal bum to lie in.

"Do not worry for Mrs. Dunham. She is given to fits of drama; it is her nature. I have not come this evening to discuss her, but you."

"Me?" I asked.

"Yes. Today is your birthday, your seventeenth, yes?" I blushed and nodded. "I thought you might enjoy a token of my appreciation on your seventeenth." He presented a small package, wrapped delicately in fine paper.

"How did you know it was my birthday? I, I cannot accept this," I pushed it away.

"Listen, I have ears and eyes. I had Mrs. Dunham bring this for you from London. I told her I knew of a lovely young lady who deserved such a prize. Of course now she won't let me alone until I tell her every bit about her." He smiled and winked. "Please, open it." He pushed it into my hands.

I hesitated before un-wrapping the package. Secured neatly inside a box lined in crimson velvet was a small, feminine bottle, a delicate purple silk ribbon adorning its neck. It looked familiar. I brought it closer so that I might study it. It read, "*Au Cour, eau de parfum.*" I gasped.

"I don't know what to say, sir!" I flushed as I realized Mr. Roeing had seen me that day in the guest room as I sifted through the drawers of the vanity. He smiled.

"Eyes, and ears," he said, pointing to each. "Au cour—it is French for, 'from the heart.'"

"Thank you," I whispered. "I don't deserve this. It's too—it's too extravagant." My heart was swelling within me, and it was beyond my control. I wanted to tell him everything, how I was beginning to feel toward him, for it was all coming to me quite clearly.

"You must understand, Kate, how much you mean to me. You are a jewel." He cupped my face in his hands and kissed me softly on the cheek. The piney scent of his shaving cream and his breath on my cheek washed over me. It was too wonderful. I stiffened. Immediately he retreated.

"I'm sorry. Please, I didn't mean anything by it." He lowered his head. "I should go now." He smiled before turning away.

"Mr. Roeing! Wait!" I reached out and grasped the cuff of his sleeve. I knew I was breaking all the rules of etiquette, but then, hadn't he?

He turned and again we were face to face. I was unsure of what to do next, what to say. I took one step closer, so close I thought he might reprimand me for indecency. My heart jumped wildly about as I looked up into his eyes.

"It's the most wonderful gift I have ever been given. Thank you, again." I stood on tiptoe to return the kiss on his piney-scented cheek, my face brushing lightly against his sideburn. For an instant, whether it was only a twitch or something more, he turned his face so that our lips nearly touched. Then he put his hands on my shoulders and took a step backward, his eyes to the ground.

"Good night, Kate," he whispered before turning and walking away once more.

I thought of the consequences that may follow my action with anyone but Mr. Roeing if I was found to be indecent. What would have happened if we had—kissed? I dared admit to myself it was what I wanted.

For a long time I stood there shaking in the wake of whatever had just occurred. Maybe if I stayed there he would return to me. There was so much I wanted to ask him. Who was he, really? Where did he come from? What did he do there? In all our tea time conversations, none of this information had been revealed, except for a vague mention that he resided in the Kent sector of London for a portion of each year.

Finally I walked back to the cottage, dabbing some perfume onto my wrist and savoring its rosiness. It would come to be as much of a comfort to me as the old swing. I stopped before the door. Mrs. Dunham had asked him if the gift she brought had something to do with Mr. Roeing's important decision. *My* gift?

Chapter Twelve

It was already October. The air was musky and fresh, and the leaves on the trees grew more colourful with each day. The time that passed since my birthday had gone on as usual. I never told Mother the full story of the perfume bottle. I suggested that Mrs. Dunham had left it behind and Mr. Roeing had given me permission to keep it. Mr. Roeing and I interacted with one another with surprising ease. Neither of us brought up what occurred the night of my birthday, but each time I thought of it I was filled with confusion.

Alas, I did not allow myself to hope. Aside from the obvious separation between us, all the signals pointed to Mr. Roeing having intentions with Josephine Bellhouse. I masked my jealousy by allowing myself more time with Ethan.

I had also much to keep my mind as for the harvesting, the canning, and all the other preparations for the annual harvest fest that Mr. Boyle conducted each year at the end of the season for all the workers. There was much food to prepare. Mother had already set about brewing the cider and had long before fashioned a giant wheel of cheese with help of our new milkmaid. Since this was one of the few times of the year that Mr. Boyle visited the estate, we wanted all to be just right. During the harvest festival he was sure to be in high spirits. I concluded it must make him feel good to brag to his friends of his generosity toward his employees.

Despite heavy cloud cover that could have ruined our day, everyone, it seemed, was jolly the day of the festival, even Joseph. An extra bonus to Mother and I was that, now that the harvest was over, Mr. Roeing had instructed several of the Hodges to re-thatch our cottage roof! We could not thank him enough for this generosity. He had even commissioned Joseph to take part. Once again I marveled at Mr. Roeing.

In the final hours before the thatching was complete, Mr. Roeing sent the men back to town to get cleaned up before the bonfire. He stayed behind to finish, for he did not wish us to go to sleep that night with a hole above our heads, and under threat of rain. He talked with me as I took some of the laundry down from the line, it being wash day. Mother was in the kitchen.

"I have heard wild tales of these harvest festivals, Kate."

"Oh, yes! I have many stories to tell. Mainly when I was small I would watch from behind a tree; I was not allowed to participate until I was much older. You'll be amazed at the bonfire. I know there will be another in town in November for Guy Fawkes Day, but our bonfires always rival it. Generally we don't retire until the last flame has died out. One year we even stayed awake to watch the sunrise!"

Mr. Roeing came down from the roof. "A few more hours and it will be in perfect condition. At least the last hole has been patched."

"It's so very good of you to do this for us, Mr. Roeing. Mother can't stop going on about it. She finds you amazing!"

"Well, she's a kind and beautiful woman. The best."

I was touched by his words. I lifted the basket to my hip and carried it into our cottage. Mr. Roeing followed, and stood watching as I draped a sheet across the table to fold it. I had a mind to ask him if and when he would be leaving us, but the truth was I did not wish to disturb our time together, however long it might be.

"Kate, there is one thing I would like to address with you." I tensed, wondering if he was going to give his notice just then, or bring up our rendezvous in the dark.

"What is it?" I asked.

"I wanted to—well how shall I say this? There is a Hodge on the farm, a Mick." He scratched his ear absentmindedly as he said it. I looked down at my folding.

"Ethan?"

"Yes, Ethan. He is a decent enough fellow, as far as I can tell. But one can never be certain, and a vagabond is not the sort of fellow that is known for his high morality." Now his hands were in his pockets.

"What are you getting at, sir?" I asked, my eyes steady on my task.

"I've noticed you with him more and more. I want you to be careful."

I continued folding, now with vigour.

"Kate, are you hearing me? The festival, the wine, the celebrating, all of it leads me to be concerned for your welfare. You are still quite young."

"I am older than Josephine Bellhouse, and many would call her eligible."

"Miss Bellhouse? We're not speaking of her, and anything Ethan might do has nothing to do with courtship or eligibility. He's a traveling farmhand, and if he desires to be with you it is not for the sake of courtship. Do not fool yourself." I dropped the laundry and turned to face Mr. Roeing directly.

"Is this about my ignorance, sir, or that he's a Mick?"

He blinked repeatedly. "Neither! I only mean that you should keep your eyes open."

"My eyes are open, sir. I see what you are getting at. A poor farm girl, and a poor farm boy—neither has a chance in the world at a decent marriage, and being that one is a Mick he cannot possibly be trustworthy. I already know of what you speak. Please, take your advice and give it to Miss Bellhouse. Live happily ever after on your glorious estates while the Mick and I have a romp in the barn. You would think differently of me if you knew—"

Mr. Roeing stepped forward and studied my eyes. I was breathing heavily now.

"Is that what you think? Do you really believe that of me? Haven't I always treated you with the utmost respect and care?"

I blinked back tears. I wished he had kept his respect and care to himself.

"Yes, sir," I whispered. He seemed pained at my answer.

"I only wish for you to be cautious—there is no harm in that. And if you think you are poor, you are mistaken."

AT LAST THE CELEBRATION was commencing. Mother and I brought out the bread and cakes and the great wheel of cheese and the barrel of cider. Mr. Boyle appeared in the late afternoon with the much anticipated barrel of wine.

Not long after, the Hodges streamed in one by one, many of them with other migrant working girls hanging casually on their arms. When the bonfire was ignited the crowd raged with delight. This, I knew, was the influence of the first round of wine. Some of the boys brought in old fiddles and began playing merry tunes while the crowd began to dance.

Mr. Roeing was subject to Mr. Boyle's company throughout the evening and so was not able to participate as much as he might have liked. But this worked to my advantage, for I was able to spend much of the night near Ethan.

When he pulled me up to dance to the fiddle, it was the first time I had danced with a man. I felt alive and unencumbered. I was so caught up in the moment that I did not notice Mr. Roeing and Mother watching us. Nor did I notice Ethan taking swigs from his flask, or the gads of indecent behaviour happening all around me.

Ethan nudged me with his flask. "Here, drink this," he urged. But I had no need for whisky; I was already giddy from his attention. I looked into his eyes. They were intent and electric, dancing as the firelight. They were hungry eyes; hungry for me. Maybe it was for this reason that I allowed him to escort me away from the bonfire. I barely noticed what had happened until we were a good distance away.

"Where are we going?" I asked, giggling. Ethan smiled and pulled me behind a great tree. I barely made out the sounds of the party, floating airily behind us like an afterthought in the night. Ahead there was only darkness but for the few streams of moonlight that managed to squeeze their way through the treetops. Suddenly I felt the roughness of a tree trunk pressing into my back. Ethan moved in closer.

"What are you doing?" I asked. My heart pounded within me. He smiled and kissed my neck sloppily as a dog devouring a bone. The essence on his breath of soured liquor and cheese was revolting.

"Wait, stop!" I shouted, and pushed him away. He grabbed my hands.

"C'mon, Katie," he spoke softly, "It's our last night together. Tell me ya won't send me away wantin' for yer love!"

"I don't know what you mean!"

"'Ave you been leadin' me on all this time? You 'afta know your eyes make a man weak at the knees, your hair—" he stroked my hair, which had loosened quite a bit with the dancing, and leaned in to kiss me. I twisted away.

"Ethan, please! This is not my experience."

He laughed. "Only one of us needs 'at. Calm down." He stroked my cheek and whispered in my ear, "Don't believe what they tell ya; it'll only hurt if ya don't cooperate."

I jerked myself away but Ethan caught me and slammed me against the tree. My head bounced off its surface. I would not notice the pain—or the blood—until later. I prayed under my breath in that moment that Jesus would help me. I gathered up all the faith I'd collected over the years. Suddenly a calm assurance came over me. I would be all right; I knew it.

I dared look him in the eye and insisted he unhand me.

For a moment he stopped. Then he laughed and slowly lifted my skirts, enjoying the control. My breath quickened. Just as I was about to scream for help, a familiar voice sounded from the darkness.

"Let her go, you filthy bastard!" Mr. Roeing shouted.

I calmed somewhat at his voice, but after realizing the way I'd been discovered I turned my head away out of shame.

Ethan looked to see who was speaking. Then a sly grin spread over his face.

"Ah, it's the master! Surely ye don't mind if I request a bit of privacy just now?"

"You're drunk. Let her go, you have no business with her."

"I'm afraid you're embarrassin' the lady, sir. We was just 'avin' a little fun."

"Kate," he called to me, "Do you want to be alone with this boy?"

"No!" I called back.

"There, you heard her. Let her go."

Ethan reluctantly released me and stepped back with his palms out in surrender. I scurried away. Mr. Roeing came closer, and now I could clearly see his eyes. There was rage behind them.

"You'd better find your way back to town now, boy." Ethan shook his head, then laughed. He took a few steps then turned back to face Mr. Roeing.

"I see what's 'appenin'." He leaned toward Mr. Roeing. "Let me know if she was any good," he said with a wink and a surly smile.

Mr. Roeing lunged forward and punched Ethan, knocking him to the ground.

"What the bloody hell was 'at?" Ethan yelped.

"Your last installment for the season. If I ever see your face again, suffice it to say you won't be able to recognize it the next time you pass a mirror. Come, Kate, your mother is worried." He grabbed my elbow and escorted me out of the forest.

The walk back seemed an eternity, for we passed it in silence. I truly wished to thank him, but shame kept the words back. His grasp on my arm was gentle but firm. Was he angry? I could not gauge his mindset.

We bypassed the dying bonfire, where several of the party were still carrying on in drunken hysterics. I saw Mother in the background and for a second our eyes met. She appeared tired and hurt. At the door to the cottage I wept. Mr. Roeing put his hand on my shoulder and noticed there was blood on the back of my head.

"My God, Kate! Didn't I warn you?" I turned, wrapped my arms around him, sobbed into his shoulder.

"Kate, the world is full of them, you must know that, lying in wait for any foolish girl to happen along."

"I'm sorry," I whispered and let go of him. When I turned from him he stepped in front of me and lifted my chin.

"Look at me." I did. He searched my eyes, then shook his head and turned from me. "Have your mother look at that wound," he said wearily.

"But wait!"

"Kate, I saved your honour tonight. Never forget that!" he called behind him as he slammed the door.

I climbed onto my bunk and wondered how long my grandmother would allow me to stay at Holmsbridge.

Chapter Thirteen

I had risen early to deliver my letter to the Post. No need to risk putting it in the mailbag for everyone's eyes to see.

Though my head was still throbbing and my thinking encumbered by the former night, I was somehow able to pen the letter to my grandmother. After returning, I spent the day tersely peeking 'round each corner of Chatworthy House, anticipating a run-in with Mr. Roeing. As it happened, I did not see him until tea time.

Once the most cherished part of the day for me, this day I rigidly sat down and poured myself some tea. I performed the action out of rote familiarity as I watched Mr. Roeing from the corner of my eye. I could sense his un-ease with me.

Mother sensed the tension and was a good saint to keep our gathering from falling silent. She spoke of the chrysanthemums and the decisions being voted on by the citizens of Hazel Grove in the coming months. I marveled at her conversational skills under such duress. I was nearly able to forget the situation at hand: until I was addressed.

Without looking up from applying Devonshire cream to his scone, Mr. Roeing uttered something so unexpected that I dropped the spoon with which I had been stirring my tea. The clang was unsettling. I steadied my hands.

"I saw you in town this morning, Kate." He had said ever so calmly.

"Did you?" I replied, attempting to sound natural after my mishap. "How is that?" I turned my head to him enough to be respectful without looking directly at him.

"Perhaps *you* should inform *me*. You were coming from the Post."

"Yes, I was," I admitted.

Poor Mother! I had thrown her into the center of it. I had not told her about the letter. I was waiting for the right time. I could see she was unsure whether she should remain to hear this. She kept her eyes focused on her teacup.

"Have you no explanation? Had I known you had business there I could have seen to it for you."

"I did not foresee that you would be going to town this morn, sir. I meant no disrespect; I was only sending a reply to my grandmother. She has requested my company to help cheer her in her season of mourning. She has asked that I arrive mid

115

November. I am not sure how long I will be. Mother is quite capable of fulfilling my duties now that harvest has passed."

Mother shifted uneasily in her chair.

"Hmm," said Mr. Roeing. "That *is* curious. Then you shall miss my own departure. I myself will be quitting Chatworthy House the third week of November."

Mother and I raised our heads in unison.

"Shall you be returning promptly, sir?" Mother asked with more than a bit of alarm. Mr. Roeing shifted casually in his chair.

"I have not yet come to an understanding as to what I will do. I suppose you shall be the first to be notified." I seethed at his nonchalance.

"Sir, I would not have agreed to join my grandmother had I known you would be going. It is cruel to Mother to cause her to abide alone during the holiday season."

"Be of good cheer, my dear women. It will be just as it was before I came. So much less work to fulfill in the winter season; and your mother is not alone. She does have Joseph," he said, looking into my eyes.

As though life were anything before he came.

Mother made a brave attempt to sound cheerful. "I do have Joseph," she said with a faint smile.

116

So it was settled. After tea I went about my duties numbly. Eventually I would run out of excuses to avoid Mr. Roeing. Upon passing him, I greeted him half heartedly.

"You are cross with me," he stated. I gave no reply.

"It's all right, Kate. You don't have to say anything. The situation is not as grim as it may seem. All things must come full circle." I looked up at him. He appeared benevolent. I could not be sure what he meant, but I assumed he would be returning to Chatworthy House in the coming season.

I couldn't stop myself from longing for him to stay always.

The following weeks preceding my departure were unexpectedly warm and memorable, as the first weeks we had spent together. Most notable was the final evening. Mother and Mr. Roeing made a small bonfire for us to enjoy in the crisp air, and Joseph joined us as we sat 'round it on the ground enjoying one another's company. Suddenly I had an idea.

"Let us each reveal a secret. Something we haven't spoken aloud, or at best something known only to you and your closest friends." My eyes glowed with challenge. The party did not feel my enthusiasm.

"Oh, please? It is only us four! And each of us is trustworthy. It never need pass this property. I will go first if the lot of you are cowards!"

"Yes, I think it best that you state your secret first," Mr. Roeing said. "Tell us, what wicked imaginations dart about within you?"

I took my time, for I did not truly know what to say, or what was safe to admit. I finally settled on something.

"When I was a girl, I told Mother I was going to town to sell her lemon curd, but instead I spent the day lying in the canoe where no one could see me. I ate an entire jar of the curd by the spoonful. Then I fell asleep only to awake later with a dreadful bellyache. I told Mother her curd did not sell that day and returned the remainder of the jars to the cellar."

"Naughty girl!" Mother chided. "I suppose I should follow with my own secret. You see, I saw you there in the canoe that day, eating my investment. Yet I could not punish you, for you looked so sweet lying there, licking the spoon as you hummed nursery rhymes. I could only imagine that I should have liked to do the same in your place! You do not think I could overlook your sunburned face and the empty jar hidden by the bank? Besides, I knew the guilt would eat at you."

I giggled. The guilt had indeed gotten to me. I later repented at church and worked extra hard to sell Mother's curd at market the following week.

"Joseph, what about you? What secret do you have lurking within that you cannot wait to be rid of?" I asked, though I could not imagine Joseph having any secrets at all. He put his head down for a long while until we wondered if he had drifted to sleep. Then, his admission.

"I married a wife once. She took her own life the week before our first anniversary."

"Joseph!" Mother and I whispered simultaneously. All the years he'd been living alongside us and we'd never known it. In the ensuing silence, a sensation of guilt crept over me for never thinking to ask Joseph questions, any question. I knew Mother was thinking the same. Mr. Roeing calmly went to Joseph's side and placed a hand on his shoulder, bowing his head in respect.

"What was her name?" he asked.

"W-Wilma," Joseph answered. He began to sob quietly. I did not have an idea what we should do next and I felt rotten for beginning the game, but witnessing Mr. Roeing so gently reassuring Joseph led me to tears as well.

"God bless Wilma," Mr. Roeing said quietly. He helped Joseph up and slowly escorted him to his cottage, leaving Mother and I dumbfounded in their wake. Mother retreated to the cottage without a word, but I remained. I wished to speak with Mr. Roeing. When at last he returned, he sat down beside me and gazed on the fire.

"I am so sorry," I said.

Mr. Roeing shook his head. "Joseph is quiet, even mischievous, but you've no idea the strong, kind soul he possesses. It would do you well to unearth it." He did not mean this as a rebuke. I sat and pondered this idea as I studied his face. He turned and smiled at me. It was then that I dared to admit to myself that I loved him.

"You never asked what my secret is," he said.

"I dare not. I cannot bear to hear another story of its kind." Then courage came to me to ask what I really wished to discover. "Have you ever been in love?" I asked, then paused. "Are you—in love?"

"There *is* someone; though this is not my secret," he admitted.

I resigned myself to keep from questioning further.

"My secret is that I—well, I adore porridge! I cannot seem to get enough of it!" he exclaimed dramatically.

"Oh, be serious!" I shouted, throwing a stone in his direction. He laughed and put his hands up in mock defense.

"All right, all right! In all seriousness, when I was younger I learned a secret while at Eton Boy's College. It was just a rumour, really, and I never thought it could be true, given its nature. Further, it may not have meant anything to me if it did not involve some very established names. The notion of what one particular fellow was purported to have done was simply disgusting to me.

"Well, years passed and I was in a gathering at a gentleman's club. Among the group was the very man whose name had been attached to this incredulous rumor! Over the course of the day, he imbibed far too much gin and at my spurring I was able to confirm that this rumour was in fact a solid truth. He did not have shame at what he had done; rather he gloated."

I asked him the nature of this incredulous rumor.

"You would not believe it. It is far too illustrious," he replied.

"That is no secret!"

"Ah, but it is. Have patience. One day I may decide to reveal the whole of it to you."

"What should stop you from revealing it to me now?" I asked, pouting.

"All things are in time and purpose, Kate."

I rolled my eyes. "When I am gone I shall not want for your outbursts of wisdom," I teased. We stood together.

"Good night, sir," I said, grasping his hands as friends might. He brought my hand to his face and kissed it. I ignored the giddy sensation moving through me and squeezed his hands.

"Thank you, sir. You have been a good master to us."

"And you have been a most interesting maid-of-all-work. I shall miss you. Sleep well." We smiled and parted ways.

I would miss his kindness.

In the cottage I tried to focus on the finishing work I had yet to do on my new gloves for my journey. I stayed up far too late sewing a thin border of lace to the cuffs of my gloves. If I thought I was being fancy thereby, I would have quite an adjustment awaiting me at Holmsbridge.

Chapter Fourteen

On the train I sighed as I held the small oak tree carving Joseph had sneaked into my bag. How thoughtful he was! Beside it lay a silk sachet that contained a gold and pearl hair clip—a gift from Mr. Roeing. He, too, had hidden it amongst my belongings. The note accompanying read,

"Dearest Kate, the gold reminded me of your heart and the pearls your smile. Wear this often and remember me,

Yours, Mr. Roeing"

It seemed far too valuable to wear. What if I lost it or misplaced it? Mother's gift was an embroidered handkerchief and a large slice of butter cake, wrapped in brown paper. Though there were many fine pastries to be had at Holmsbridge, none could compare to Mother's simple cake, which contained only a few ingredients; but love most of all. I missed her dreadfully. I had no idea that staying with the Madam would lead me into near isolation.

At Glastonbury Station a carriage was awaiting me, with a footman as an escort. He rode with the driver on the perch so that the cabin would be mine alone, and I was grateful for it. Holmsbridge's gate was far less foreboding to me than the first time I'd passed through it, and I nearly felt nostalgic to see Reginald's face at the door, despite his unwillingness to feel nostalgic toward me. He escorted me directly to meet with the Madam, who was seated at a secretary's desk in her study.

She stood and looked me over, peering over her reading spectacles. "Katherine," she said, without any expression to tell on her face. "Welcome," she added, this time with a faint smile. I curtseyed.

"Thank you, madam, it's a pleasure to be back," I said.

Her demeanor was calm, yet not icy. Beyond that it was anybody's guess what she might be feeling. She was still arrayed in a black, still mourning my grandfather's death.

She expressed hope that my journey was comfortable, and I asked if she was in good health. Then, as though she was pained to continue our conversation, she called Reginald to bring in the etiquette instructor. She must have read the surprise on my face.

"It is a matter of honour. I shan't have you going about with poor posture and manners, not to mention those—looks," she explained. Then she gave the instructor full reign of me.

I was whisked off by the instructor to an iron bath tub filled with hot soapy water. Though I was confused at the pace of things, I must say a hot bath was just the thing after my journey.

There was one such bath in Chatworthy House, and I confess that once when Mr. Roeing had forgotten to pull the plug on the bath, I quickly undressed and had a bath myself. While this may seem deplorable to some, one must understand this was a luxury I had never been afforded. A little of Mr. Roeing's filth did not deter me—it was a stolen treat. Most of my bathing had taken place in the stream, or, during the winter, in a receptacle in the cellar kitchen.

Now I was being afforded my very own hot bath, and I enjoyed it until the water grew cold, and the scent of lavender permeated every pore of my body. That is, after my instructor had given her discourse on proper bathing techniques as I lay in my bare, intimidated skin.

After washing, I was issued new undergarments, which were quite to my liking. Then I was measured from tip to toe, so that the new gowns the Madam had ordered might be finished for me. I would need to grow accustomed to tight corsets. My former corset was so worn it scarcely constituted a corset anymore. My instructor saw to it that the new one was laced as tightly as possible. The fashionable bustles at the backs of the new gowns brought quite a bit of extra stress to my back, making breathing even harder. For the first week I could not take the stairs without nearly blacking out. But posture and form were of utmost importance, and so I had to endure.

My hands were a great cause for concern. They were chapped and ragged from scrubbing and the other rigorous chores of a maid—they were a sure giveaway to my station in life. After the dirt had been painfully scrubbed out from beneath my nails, reeking ointments were rubbed into my hands throughout that first day and all the next week, and I was ordered to keep them covered at all times with gloves. My teeth, which were not to standard, were brushed fiercely several times per day with soda paste, and I was given lemons to chew as a bleaching agent. This did much good, and I was pleased with the results, even if gagged in the process.

My training was furthered by quizzing on table etiquette and social matters, and lessons on diction were given so that I could speak the Queen's English with excellence. This was the easiest of my tasks, as my speech was already superior than that of the average servant, thanks to Mother.

My previous visions of glamour were clouding over with all the stipulations imposed on me. I did not understand why all the trouble was being taken to train me.

My instructor told the Madam that two weeks would not be nearly enough time to convert me into a proper lady. Six months was a far better timetable, she'd said, but the Madam was frugal, and knew that once my cousin arrived, such duties could be transferred to her.

The focus of my last day with the instructor circulated around my hair. After a few specialty rinses and many painful tries at rearranging, my hair was at last deemed, "respectable." The instructor and I both sighed in relief when the Madam gave her final approval. I collapsed into my lovely bed that night, exhausted.

Henceforth were two more days until cousin Isabella's arrival. Per my understanding, I had come to be with my grandmother in her time of mourning, yet I nary passed more than tea time with her each day. With the servants I wished I could attempt friendship, but as this was improper, and as they knew I was not a true lady I was paid less respect. Even my assigned lady in waiting, Sheila, a girl of about the same age as me, was ill at ease in my presence.

I dreaded the first event I would attend, lest I unwittingly break with convention and make a fool of myself and my family—my hosts. The two empty days awaiting Isabella seemed longer than the duration of time I had been there combined. What did one do with oneself when there were no chores?

I found myself suffering from boredom; a new sensation. Once or twice I walked about the gardens, which were by now descending into hibernation after a lengthy summer of bloom. I read through some books from my grandfather's library. I slept. I admired my newly invented persona in the mirrors (were they magic, or was that truly me?). Yet, the isolation was almost more than I could bear with its silence.

I did have garment changes to occupy a fair portion of my time. Sheila was at my service to assist me through the elaborate processes of corset tightening, buttoning, tying, and fastening in places I could not reach for myself.

I would don a gown in the morning to wear to breakfast, a gown for strolling after breakfast (this I attempted to avoid as I felt it was unnecessary), one for luncheon and tea, and still another for dinner. They were incredibly heavy and cumbersome; still, in my borrowed wardrobe were the most excellent outfits! Though I thought it a waste, since nobody was even to see me, it was my distinct pleasure to sport them. And the superior food made every other endurance far worth the exertion, not withstanding my homesickness.

With Isabella's arrival, any homesickness I had been nursing all but vanished. She would be my first ever companion of the same age. I shall never forget the moment she swept into Holmsbridge in the fashion that one might traverse the threshold between fantasy and flesh. To tell the truth, I blinked, for I was not sure if I was seeing a vision or reality.

Isabella possessed the ability to captivate the world around her, whether like a spider weaving a web or like a small girl gathering snapdragons in the sun, I was unsure. Her hair was a remarkable shade of freshly churned butter, her eyes a tumultuous and bewitching ocean. I would come to find that her conduct was equally astounding; she was an obvious force, as compelling as gravity itself. Not that she was all benevolence: those gray-blues cast a duplicitous shadow. Yet, when she turned them on me for the first time, I knew we were to get along very well, indeed.

"So this is the little tramp," she said with a sideways glance as she removed her gloves. She gave a playful smirk so that I would take no offense.

"And you must be the Nosey Parker," I answered, surprising myself as much as the others. Isabella turned to the Madam.

"Nana, just where have you put that demure cousin I was taught to expect? This girl is nothing less than a firebrand. What's this about a Nosey Parker? Is this how you refer to me in my absence?"

The Madam rolled her eyes. "All I can conclude is that your presence evokes the devil in all of us! I'll not be my customary self until you've gone. The Lord bless and keep me until then!" She lowered her voice. "Just mind the situation. This Katherine is no relation of yours, only a companion."

"Yes, Nana. You've dealt me the trajectory. I shan't be a tattle-tale." She winked at me. I marveled that the Madam tolerated the title of "Nana". Her expression even seemed to soften as Isabella said it.

"Isabella, I shall expect you to be the perfect hostess to Katherine. She has had some formal training these weeks but there is more to learn. You should have seen the vulgarity she was upon arrival! I want her thoroughly cultured; no one should think anything less of her than a young lady of established wealth. You have the remainder of the week."

Isabella laughed in a high pitched trill that was at once troubling and delightful. "A small undertaking! I suppose I should be responsible for converting the savage masses to Christianity in as little time as well!" she chided. "Upon my word, at least her wardrobe is decent. This frock I must try for myself," she said as she touched the cuff of my gown. "Shall you be affording me a few new frocks as well, Nana?"

"Child! The misery has begun! Now off you go! I shan't be obliged to see your faces until dinner. You will take tea in the solarium." Before she turned off, I thought I caught a semblance of a smile.

I followed Isabella to the Violet Room where she would be staying. So this was the coveted room! How fantastic! No wonder Mother had been envious of her sister when we had last visited Holmsbridge. The room was double the size of mine, and filled with twice the luxury. Nearly every object was a gorgeous shade of pale purple, from the curtains to the planter, which was filled with violets, no less. I had never seen its like.

Isabella wasted no time getting herself acquainted with my history. She explained how she could not attend the funeral, as she had been very ill with influenza. "Nearly didn't make it through that one," she said as she situated herself on the chaise longue. When she was quite comfortable, she urged me to speak. "Pray, go on, tell me all," she said, clasping her hands in her lap.

"What is it that you already know?" I asked uneasily.

"I know that Lord Percy is your true father, and that," she stopped and made sure there was no one else passing by the room, "that he sold your mother to another man!" Her eyes were ablaze with the forbidden knowledge. She giggled, then sobered. "So, what of this other man? Nana said he was very poor and that he passed on when you were small."

"Well, yes, all that is true. He was very poor, but he was quite a good soul. What he did for Mother, for us, well, that took an immense amount of character. I think of him as an angel."

Isabella sighed. "What is it like to be very poor? Is it dreadful?" she asked, her eyes focused in a far away place.

I laughed uneasily. "Perhaps you should try your hand at it. There is no teacher quite like experience!"

"I'm no romantic, you know. I prefer to learn vicariously. That is why I find you so fascinating."

"Why, there is not a fascinating thing about me."

"Don't you find your story to be interesting at all? If it were me I would mount a horse immediately and ride to Lord Percy's estate. There I would demand he reinstate me. Think of everything you have missed because of that bastard! And if he resisted, a bit of blackmail would need be employed. Everyone fears scandal as the plague, but I declare, a little scandal is healthy now and then. Of course, I can see you aren't the type, and I am glad for it. A scandal would only detour my own devices."

"Devices?" I asked. Isabella blinked innocently at me.

"You see, I must confess that one of the main reasons I have come is to make the acquaintance of Mr. Jonathan Percy." I gasped.

"My—my—*that* Jonathan Percy?"

"Yes, your apparent brother; *that* Jonathan. He is so handsome! If you didn't have that unfortunate attachment to him you would likely be smitten of him as well. I'd have him in my grips already if it weren't for this—petty circumstance." She shrugged as if it meant nothing.

"Isabella, it's too dangerous," I warned. "The Madam says we must go everywhere together and if he discovers—"

"Oh, Katherine, there is no use debating me. I always get what I want. You'll soon understand that. We must make certain that he will not discover. Anyways, I don't know how he would have any inkling about you to begin with. There is almost no risk at all. That is, there won't be when I get finished with you." She looked me over. "You really must get into the habit of squaring your shoulders. Let me have a look at your hands. I hear they are treacherous!"

I sat up straight and removed my gloves. My hands were far from the disaster they had been when I arrived, but they still needed time to heal. Isabella clucked her tongue and shook her head. I replaced the gloves.

"The Madam said that you would escort me to town to purchase a new set of gloves."

"Did she? Then she will be caring for the bill as well! We shall go first thing in the morning. But do learn to mask your feelings. Your countenance is as plain as a tawdry advertisement. You're a magnet for query."

The Madam was right—life would not be customary until Isabella had gone.

Chapter Fifteen

The following afternoon was my first venture outside of Holmsbridge since I had come. The Madam had allowed us to go to town with Sheila as our chaperone. I enjoyed myself tremendously as we passed through town in our carriage, watching the bustling activity on the streets and pointing excitedly at the city's monuments. But Isabella was not interested in architecture. Boutiques were her hand.

As we strolled through the streets, it was as if I were being seen for the first time. No longer invisible, I was unsure how to react to all the kindnesses being paid me in the form of friendly greetings and hat tipping, the hat tipping generally directed at my beautiful blonde counterpart. One gentleman even opened a door for us. Clearly Isabella was accustomed to this type of treatment, and coolly curtseyed. I followed suit.

She then bought me a lovely brooch at a small shop, and after we went to take tea in an exclusive teahouse. Sheila, of course, stayed behind in the carriage.

In the teahouse the scents of exotic tea, French perfume, and buttery biscuits seduced my senses. I tried to mask my glee as I took in the affluent clientele sitting on tufted settees beside the tables, sipping their tea from the finest bone china. This felt to me like espionage. Eyes such as mine were not supposed to behold such loveliness.

We were seated near the window. I sat admiring the intricately patterned linens at our table. "These are silk!" I whispered to Isabella regarding the table napkins. She rolled her eyes.

"Yes. You giddy thing! Mind your environment." I apologized and made my best effort to appear nonchalant, even as the framed masterpieces on the wall begged for my open admiration. As wonderful as Holmsbridge was, this place had an extra air of glamour that I could not resist. Just as I had truly secured my emotions, a string quartet began a bittersweet ensemble near the entrance. Isabella sent me a glance of warning.

An attendant brought our tea service immediately. "We'll take the Moroccan blend," Isabella said, and the lady disappeared into the back.

"So, Katherine, word has it that this brother of yours has just returned from a journey to America. Isn't that exciting?"

"How is it that you know?"

"I make it my business to know such things."

The lady brought the Moroccan blend, as well as a triple-tiered plate of biscuits, pastries, and berries.

"Watch yourself," she warned as my eyes lusted after the feast, "too many of those and your clothing will cease to fit properly." I was unaccustomed to the concept of weight gain, but since my arrival at Holmsbridge my figure had grown more plump. This was a positive on my too-thin frame. However, since I did not carry out any manual duties, I would need to be more careful of my eating habits. I reluctantly pushed away a luscious tart of lemon crème. Instead, I sipped on the wonderfully refreshing tea that was flavoured with mint.

"Tell me your plans, Isabella, for I can see that you are scheming even presently." I congratulated myself on my speech. I was sounding more a lady all the time.

"Wait a few moments and you shall see for yourself."

"While we wait let's talk about your parents. How are they? I mean, how can they be described?"

Isabelle appeared bored with the topic and surveyed the room as she spoke.

"Oh, I suppose they are comparable to any other parents. I don't see them often. Father enjoys a good day of hunting, and

Mother is always in London, it seems. She fancies herself a painter. It's a foolish past time. She isn't even any good at it."

"And you? What do you do with your days?"

"Whatever do you mean?"

I was unsure of how to elaborate, so I changed the topic. "Mother says that your mother is a viper!" I whispered. Isabella laughed.

"Is that so? If that is true than your mother is—well, it isn't kind. I shan't say. Then again, I suppose Mother *is* rather a viper. A temper, you know; spoilt. Nana always favoured her. I should like to become acquainted with the infamous Victoria. Is she as sensual as they say?"

"Sensual? Not in the least."

Isabella stirred her tea loftily. "The rumour mill is quite delicious, even if it is inaccurate at times. I only meant that your mother had the capability of attracting more than a few suitors in her time. I suppose that is why no one would question a story involving a love affair."

I shrugged. "Do you think I resemble my—father?" Isabella looked me over with squinted eyes. "I've only seen him once or twice. I suppose your eyes are reminiscent of him."

Just then an especially stylish pair of young ladies from another table stood and walked our way. Isabella winked at me, and I knew this to mean these ladies were a part of her scheme.

I straightened my posture and tried to appear as demure as possible.

"Is it you, Isabella Davis?" asked the tallest one with the black hair. She glanced suspiciously at me, then back at Isabella.

"Why, Helen and Mary-Therese! How *are* you ladies faring? Won't you join us?"

"We really haven't the time to spare, thank you. How is your grandmother?"

"Well, thank you, though she longs for her time of mourning to end."

"And who is this keeping your company?"

"Forgive me, this is a friend of mine, Miss Katherine Thurgood."

"How do you do Miss Thurgood," they said in unison.

I returned the greeting. I wasn't sure I was fond of them, and I could see they felt similarly.

"Well, it is best that we be on our way now," said the shorter one with the blonde hair. "Isabella, why don't you come by this Saturday? Helen and I are hosting a social at her estate. The hunting season is such a bore. You could bring your— friend." Already she'd forgotten my name.

"A social? Why, Katherine and I would be delighted to attend."

"Good. We shall see you Saturday at three o'clock. Ta ta." The two turned and floated on.

"Those girls are joined at the hip," Isabella whispered when they were out of hearing range. "They come here most days at tea time. If there were only one social to attend it would be theirs. Everyone who is anyone will be there, including Jonathan Percy."

I might have made a fuss over her plans, but I was beginning to warm to the thrill of espionage. How exciting to look danger in the face!

Isabella's mouth dropped open. "And speak of the devil..."

Before I saw him outside the window coming toward the teahouse, she had started toward the door. I would have been content to let her go out alone if she had not returned to take me by the hand with a yank.

"Keep your head down!" she whispered, then pretended to carry on a conversation with me. As we neared she purposely bumped into him.

"Miss, please forgive me! How careless of me to not mind where I am going," Jonathan apologized.

"Oh, I *am* sorry," Isabella said in a very sweet voice. "It is I who has caused this catastrophe." I wondered if Jonathan detected her coyness. The young man beside Jonathan spoke.

"Hello, Miss Davis."

"Mr. Jacob Burton? Is it you indeed?" she asked innocently.

"Yes. It has been so long since we last spoke. How is your family?"

"They fare well, and yours?"

Jonathan interjected. "Jacob, you didn't tell me you knew of such a lovely young lady. What brings you here, Miss Davis?"

"Why, we've only just met," she flirted. "I see no need to reveal all."

"I can only guess that she presently visits her grandmother, Lady Braithwaite," Jacob Burton said drily. My stomach dropped. Isabella pouted at his reticence to play along.

"Lady Braithwaite!" Jonathan exclaimed. "How is she faring in her time of mourning? And how is it that I was not informed of this family connection?"

"My grandmother is well. I am not sure of the latter question. I know exactly who *you* are, Mr. Percy," she said. Jacob rolled his eyes.

Jonathan happened to catch my eye in that moment. He paused before addressing me. "Hello, I believe we have met." I could not open my mouth to answer.

"This is my good friend, Miss Katherine Thurgood," Isabella answered for me. "You can't have met her, she has never been to Somerset in all her life."

"No, I am sure we have met, perhaps during Season in London? Mayfair, perhaps?"

"I'm afraid not," I managed to say. I could feel my cheeks filling with hot blood. Our faces were not so dissimilar. His colouring was lighter than mine, but there above his left brow was a mole, as above my own!

"Then where does your family hail from, if I may inquire?"

"I don't suppose you've met any of them. They are the reclusive sort," Isabella interjected.

"I suppose not," Jonathan mused.

"Anyway, I am sure you will both be attending the social this Saturday. There we can get more acquainted. I'm just dying to hear all about your adventures in America, Mr. Percy." He looked at her with marvel.

"Gentlemen," she said as she curtseyed. I curtseyed as well, and on we walked. "Don't look back," she whispered under her breath. "Let *them* watch *us*."

Once in the carriage, I scolded Isabella. Looking danger in the face was not as fulfilling as I had hoped it would be.

"What was all that? If he tells his father—*our* father—"

"Wasn't that divine?" she interrupted. "I didn't even plan on crossing paths with him. I only guessed I would see him at Helen's social, and yet there he was in plain sight!" I didn't tell her that Jonathan and I had met once before. I hoped my transformation was enough to mask my former appearance.

"Is something the matter with you that you are so willing to risk the scandal?" I spat.

"Katherine, you must relax. The social will be loads of fun! You'll see. Jacob Burton was once a beau of mine, you know," she said proudly. "Actually, he is Mary-Therese's brother. He is handsome, but such a bore. I can see Jonathan is far more interesting."

"This is my brother we speak of!"

"Quiet yourself, girl! If there is a scandal, you will be long gone before anything is to happen. Anyway, what *could* happen? Some questions are raised? Neither party would admit relation to your mother."

My heart sank. Was I nothing more in this world than a social experiment? I felt a pang for Mother, and another for Mr. Roeing. "All things must come full circle," he'd said. I wasn't sure what he meant, but I direly hoped he would be returning to Chatworthy House, and soon.

My house of cards seemed fit to tumble.

Chapter Sixteen

"Girls! Girls!" cried the Madam as we entered the dining room for dinner. She sat waving an invitation of some sort.

"Do sit down. I have quite an important announcement to make!" She was grinning widely. This was the first I had seen of her teeth. It seemed inappropriate to look upon them, as it is inappropriate to openly gaze upon a thigh exposed, or into the eyes of the Queen.

"Do you know what this is, my loves? This is a highly coveted invitation. Only the finest are invited to an event such as this. This year, we have been named among them! In two weeks we have been called to attend a Christmas ball at the home of the honourable Duke of Berkshire!"

Isabella squealed. "Nana! How wonderful!"

"I don't know how this has come to be, but it is a marvelous honour! Now, as His Grace resides in another district, I am not feeling fit to travel the distance in my age; and in mourning besides. Katherine will be attending in my place." She looked at me with steely eyes. "I can trust you, can't I, Katherine? This is an incredible opportunity, and though you will not be addressed as one of us, you will be representing us still." Without looking away, she asked Isabella, "How is Katherine performing in her office?"

"Well, Nana. No one suspects a thing; although she could improve on her assertion."

"Excellent, then I trust this social on Saturday will be useful for practicing more at her social skills, and you must do your best to school her in dance. I want you to practice with her each day. "Katherine," she said, turning again to me, "do you know who the Duke of Berkshire is?" I shook my head no.

"He is a close associate to the Queen herself, or rather her late husband, Prince Albert. A duke is highest in rank in the peerage of nobility in our great nation; he sits just beneath royalty. There exist only around a dozen men in this station: we are talking of an extremely powerful man. He is certainly the nearest thing to royalty we may ever have the pleasure of encountering. Represent us well." It was both a suggestion and a threat.

Needless to say, dinner was difficult to get through. The idea of a real ball sounded spectacular! The seamstress arrived the following morning to have us measured for our ball gowns, and by Saturday the gowns were delivered for the initial fitting. Isabella chose a gauze in pale blue, and I a daring crimson tulle with yards of extra fabric to make a trailing bustle.

I brought my lady Sheila along to the Violet Room so that Isabella and I could ready ourselves for the social. There I came upon a most unsettling scene.

"You lazy cow! I told you I wanted the gray gown!" Isabella shouted at her lady. When she spied me at the door her expression changed instantly into a smile. I was weary of the manner in which the servants were treated in this new world.

"You needn't call her a cow, or lazy, for that matter. She works quite capably for you," I found the courage to say. The room's climate turned wintry in the blink of an eye.

"Oh, well I suppose you *would* have feelings for the little imps," she spat. I clenched my jaw as Sheila helped me undress.

"Really, why is that?" I asked.

"Birds of a feather."

"I would rather be an imp than to view the world from the tip of my nose. It must be frigid up there," I said as I smoothed my hair in the mirror. I wanted to bring our shared bloodline into the discussion, and I would have, if not for the servants. No one was to know that piece of information.

"When I said to improve on your assertion I didn't mean that you should exercise it on me," was Isabella's final, pouty word.

We remained cool with one another even as the carriage arrived at Helen's estate.

The atmosphere at the social was jovial, and less formal than I was expecting. The Siamese twins met us at the door and led us into the drawing room where a group was playing charades. I was much more comfortable after scanning the room and finding no trace of Jonathan Percy. Mary-Therese offered us each a glass of punch, which I later learned had been spiked with mulberry wine. Luckily I only sipped from it. The charade was easy; the chap motioning crazily at the center of the room was pretending to be King Arthur. I dared not blurt the answer among a group of strangers. Isabella was not so encumbered.

At the sound of her voice, the entire room fell silent and turned to look at her. Had she that much of an effect on people? She was obviously pleased with the attention.

"Might I have a turn? I have a most delicious charade!" she said. She did not await validation, but made her way to the center of the room. I could see the men were captivated with her, and the women, those who did not know her, were in a private frenzy over what to do about her. Some of them began whispering, but as soon as she began the charade, all seemed to favour her. I was more relaxed in that moment than I had been for days; until Jonathan Percy appeared at my side.

"Miss Thurgood, how do you do?" he greeted with a bow. I curtseyed in return.

"Well, and yourself, Mr. Percy? I was not aware of your presence this afternoon." I fidgeted with my petticoat as I looked to Isabella for direction, but she was not looking our way.

"I have been discussing some business with a colleague in the smoking room." I found the word colleague to be indulgent for such a young chap. I saw Isabella look up at us in a panic, which she quickly masked. She gracefully abandoned her audience and made her way toward us.

"I believe there is something you may wish to confess to me, Miss Thurgood."

"Really? And to what might I wish to confess?" I asked, attempting to avoid giving answer.

"Mr. Percy, I daresay my afternoon might have been ruined if I weren't to see your face!" Isabella interjected. "You are a ray of sunshine, brightening up the room as you do. Don't forget—you promised to tell me all the dirty details of your journey to the United States. Let's take a stroll, shall we?" She entwined her arm in his.

"Actually, I was only just finishing up with Miss Thurgood." Isabella shot me a jealous glance before shifting her expression again.

"I really don't know how long we will be staying on," she said, tugging at his arm. "Please, tell me just a smidgen, and after you can finish up with her." Jonathan would not budge.

From the other end of the parlour our hostess announced that a quadrille dance was commencing. A fellow sat down at the piano to play a tune as the furniture was cleared away and the party formed into sets. At least this was a dance I was familiar with. However, my familiarity was more by sight than experience, though Isabella had practiced it with me a few times that week.

Jonathan's friend Jacob Burton appeared at Isabella's side and shyly requested a dance with her. She glanced pleadingly at Jonathan.

"Jacob, I regret to inform you that I have already paired up with Miss Davis," Jonathan said for her sake.

Jacob hung his head for a moment, and then as the second quadrille was lacking one couple, I became his next choice. I accepted his invitation so as not to cause him embarrassment, but the truth was I was so terrified that I would miss a step and look the fool that I considered feigning a knee injury.

As we danced, I thought of how masterfully I was getting on. During the dance Jonathan met my eyes more than once, with an expression I might describe as perturbed. I lost my concentration. Was it I he was perturbed with, or was accommodating Isabella the cause? Alas, a feigned injury was now unnecessary: I twisted my ankle.

When Jacob and I stepped out, I was pleased that the dance went on smoothly without us. Had the party stopped for my sake, it would have made matters all the more embarrassing for me. Our quadrant was filled immediately by another couple.

As I looked up to thank Jacob for escorting me to a chaise, I was shocked to find it was not Jacob, but Jonathan. I must have missed the details, but when I looked up, I saw Jacob dancing with an entirely miffed Isabella. I wondered at the oddity of it all before directing my attention to the intent eyes of Jonathan Percy.

"Thank you, Mr. Percy. You are most kind," I offered, and averted my eyes.

As he propped my foot on a stool his eyes continued to search after mine. When there was nothing left for him to do I could not help but ask him why he was looking at me so.

"Because, I recall where I have seen you."

"Where, pray tell?" I asked, breathless.

"At Longhurst, of course," he said impatiently. "Why did you not admit it? I saw you the day of Lord Braithwaite's funeral. You curiously showed up at my door with another lady. Am I to assume she is your mother? Or is she your employer? You were not dressed then as you are now." When I did not answer he continued.

"We haven't much time. The dance will end in moments! Be forthcoming with me. I sense this is important."

"Please, do not think me rude, as there are many things I am not permitted to reveal. It was a mistake for me to come here today."

"I am only interested in one thing—who was that woman? Dash it! I can't recall her name, but the mention of it to Father had quite an affect on his sensibilities. Tell me, what is her name? Is she your mother?"

"I regret that I cannot inform you of it. Why is it so imperative that you know all of this?"

"There is some piece of very consequential information in it and I intend to discover it!"

"Then you do so at your own peril."

"Her name! What is it?" he spat, his hand holding to my wrist. I could see the quadrilles splitting up and knew that Isabella would waste no time intervening.

"Her name is Victoria, and that is all the information you shall obtain from me. Be wary; I do not envy the person who dares mention her name in your father's presence. Know that in doing so you endanger me, and though I am a stranger to you I ask that you consider my welfare."

"What have you to do with my father?"

"Well, well, how is that ankle?" asked Isabella, by now more than a bit disenchanted. Her sweet overtone failed to disguise her smoldering ire, and I feared her eyes would burn through my flesh.

"Forgive me, Miss Davis, for abandoning you just then. Jacob preferred to have the dance with you, and as you can see, all is well here." Suavely he escorted Isabella away by the elbow. "And now, about my travels to the United States..."

I sighed in relief. I doubt I had taken a breath at all during the conflict. Soon the party migrated my way as one by one the curious arrived to have a chat with the injured one. This must be how it felt to be a celebrity. Isabella made sure that Jonathan and I did not cross paths anymore that afternoon by keeping him quite to herself.

My ankle was well on its way to healing by the time we arrived back at Holmsbridge, and my spirits were high, although lingering was an ill sensation at the pit of my stomach concerning the conversation with Jonathan. I attempted to pass it from my mind and set my sights toward the ball we would be attending soon. Our gowns would be delivered the following morning and I could not wait to see them.

"It appears we shall be having our final fittings tomorrow!" Isabella said in a singsong voice as we entered the foyer. Alas, we heard Reginald's footsteps approaching, and I knew that with them came the promise of some measure of doom or another. He stepped before me and bowed. In his hand was a letter.

"For you, Miss Thurgood," he said.

"Thank you, Reginald," I said, and took it. He disappeared like a ghost.

"What is it?" Isabella asked.

I recognized Mother's handwriting. "It's from my mother." I read it quickly and concealed it. "She's well. She was writing to tell me about her plans for the holiday," I lied. "Listen, we had best retire early tonight. Tomorrow we will have our final fittings and then you promised to help me decide how to arrange my hair."

Isabella took the bait more readily than I hoped, and soon I was in the Blue Room alone. I flopped onto the settee. What would I do now?

The letter hadn't been about holiday plans. Unfortunately, it was about Mr. Boyle. When he discovered I was to be away for more than a fortnight he was angered with me. In his mind, neglecting to ask his permission to go was an act of disobedience that he could not forgive. I would no longer be permitted to return to Hazel Grove, or at least to the farm.

Oh, Mr. Roeing! How I wished I could contact him. Perhaps he could intervene. Where was I to go? I could not tell the Madam or Isabella. I knew this would only bring additional dishonour toward us in their eyes. Somewhere in the bowels of the early morning I decided what I would do.

My options were as follows: I could request more time with the Madam and try to attach myself to her, or I could request to leave early and she would arrange train fare for me. I could use the train ticket to go home or to another city and attempt to hire myself out as a servant. I had no training or education to do otherwise. This prospect brought with it the possibility of being underfed and treated poorly, not to mention that I had no money on which to live while I searched for work. I knew I hadn't the courage to subject myself to the unknown.

I must find a suitor at the ball.

Chapter Seventeen

We couldn't find an adequate piece of jewelry to fit with my gown. With my gloves, a thin strand of pearls round my wrist was a nice complement, but the Madam and Isabella insisted I needed something more. None of the selected brooches seemed to fit. Then the realization flooded me—Mr. Roeing's gift would make the perfect accessory. I unearthed it from my belongings and brought it to the ladies.

"It's perfect! Where did you get such a piece?" the Madam questioned. I fidgeted. How was I to explain?

"It was a gift. From our employer," I stated.

"Is this employer unusually wealthy? I don't imagine a piece such as this generally finds its way into hamlets such as yours."

"Yes, I realize," I said, though I had not realized. "Our employer's wife passed away many years ago and her belongings only brought him the remembrance of her death, so he passed them 'round."

I felt bad for stretching the truth. They studied me, deciding whether or not I had stolen it, I suppose. This made me wonder where Mr. Roeing could have recovered it. He'd said it reminded him of me, but to my knowledge there was not a fine jewelry shop near Hazel Grove. Had he taken a journey in the night while we were asleep? It must have come with Mrs. Dunham, I concluded.

"Well, how very generous of him. It is the perfect match," Isabella said as she took it and fastened it into my hair. "Come, we haven't much time before the carriage is ready, and I have yet to find a piece for my gown."

Sifting through the Madam's jewels was a dream. She had superb pieces made from every gem and precious metal known to man, from brooches to necklaces, hair pieces, and bracelets. I wondered about their combined worth. Isabella selected a brooch with a large pearl center, which was encased in a border of small diamonds. I understood she felt the need to trump me. She looked stunning, yet when I looked at my own reflection I could not deny that I was stunning as well.

My plan did not seem so unattainable.

During the long carriage ride Isabella took the opportunity to repeat all the rules regarding proper ballroom behavior.

"You must not refuse to dance with any gentleman that asks you, unless you have first agreed to dance with another. Not ever! You mustn't injure the feelings of anyone. If word reaches the host that you have done so, this is expressly disagreeable and the blame will land on the head of the Braithwaite family. You don't wish to be labeled ill-mannered, do you?" She paused to look at me, then continued. "You must not quit the ballroom alone, nor cross the ballroom floor on your own. You and I must be with a female escort at all times that is married. My mother will be in attendance so we needn't fret about that."

"Your mother? Your mother will be there? Does she know?"

"Yes, of course," she said with a wave of her hand. "I cannot guarantee that she will be anything more than civil to you. Her rivalry with your mother runs deep." I put my hand to my brow out of anxiousness. "Continuing on, you mustn't talk a great deal while dancing—"

"Yes, I know, and I should have my head tilted outward at all times with a look of gaiety on my face. This you have divulged numerous times; though I don't foresee that I will need to use any of this information."

"You will need it. Under the watchful eye of Society all is kept under surveillance. There shall be many wanting a dance with you."

"Truly?"

"Do you realize with whom you attend? The Braithwaites and Davis' are well-known. In that gown you'll have quite a few interests, though I don't suppose anyone will garner as many names as I. Anyways, it wouldn't be proper of the manager of the dance to allow any lady to go without a dance partner. The next rule of thumb is not to boast to the less fortunate ladies about how many dances you've had."

My trepidation was mounting by the moment, especially at the thought of having to entertain as many gentlemen as she was alluding to.

"Now, you mustn't show one gentleman more favour in your dancing than another, it looks vulgar; and never accept refreshments from a gentleman with whom you aren't already well acquainted."

"But at Helen's social I took refreshments from someone I was unacquainted with."

"Yes, that was a private party. The rules are all changed for a ball. Now, on we go. Do not allow any gentleman with whom you are not acquainted to sit beside you, and only with your permission can an acquaintance do so, though I don't see that you shall come upon any acquaintance this evening. Remember, if you are asked about your family line, you will tell them your father has interests in America." Isabella sighed and clasped her hands, dropping them in her lap. "And that is about all there is to know."

When she had finished, she was truly finished, and had nothing at all more to say. It seemed hours when at last a marvelous scene appeared in the coach window. It was a castle! A real castle! Rising out of its setting like a glorious ship in the distant sea, it took my breath from me.

"Is that it? It's a castle! Are we at Buckingham Palace?"

Isabella guffawed at my ignorance. "Heavens no! We are a hundred kilometers from there. This is Roeing Oaks, though it isn't a castle at all, only a large manor house. It is marvelous, isn't it?" I choked at her words.

"What did you just say?"

"Roeing Oaks. This is where the ball is to take place. Don't you recall?"

"You only said we were going to a ball at the home of the Duke of Berkshire. It can't be..." I whispered.

"Yes, this is where the Duke of Berkshire resides, and it's formally known as Roeing Oaks. Now, remember, the Duke is to be addressed, 'Your Grace'. This you mustn't forget!" She looked over at me to find me staring blankly ahead. I could not believe the words I had just heard.

"Katherine, what ever is the matter?"

"It's just that name, Roeing. Who—who is it?"

"Drat if I know; probably the name of one of the ancestors that built the place, or a landowner."

I clasped Isabella's hand as we pulled behind a line of carriages. Slowly we rolled along a lane lined with great oak trees on either side, whose branches formed a canopy above us. How exquisite! Even as the leaves had gone for winter to reveal bared branches, it was somehow still lush.

When we came out of the lane our carriage rolled up behind a line of others. The grounds were now more clearly visible, and the castle was even more breathtaking as we neared. We watched as one by one the guests were escorted out of the carriages. I marveled at the parade of prestige all around me. At last it was our turn to be escorted out of our carriage. We stood looking up at the cascading stairs that lead toward the entry.

"Follow my every move, and for heaven's sake keep your face straight!" she warned. I rolled my shoulders back as I had been taught, and fixed on my face the straightest expression I could manage. We walked up the steps and into the foyer, which was bustling with people. As wraps and greatcoats were collected I took in the surroundings. The foyer was marvelously decked in evergreen boughs and holly and red ribbons. Colourful glass ornaments were woven into them, and the glow of candlelight rounded out the atmosphere to give it a jovial holiday feel.

An elaborate dance card, trimmed with red ribbon and lace, was handed to us each.

"We must locate my mother before we enter," Isabella instructed. A man stood at the ballroom's entryway and announced each arrival as they entered.

"There she is," Isabella said, tilting her head.

I could only hope she meant the stone-faced lady with the ridiculous patch of feathers protruding from the back of her outlandish hairstyle. Mother would not believe what I would tell her. Alas, this was the viper herself, Aunt Betina.

We approached.

There is no kind way to interpret her expression when first she saw me. She must have mistaken me for a garden slug—the disgust was apparent. Yet I can't say the expression she awarded her daughter was terribly warm either. She did not utter a word, but nodded in greeting, and a second nod was given to signal that we follow behind her.

The handsome gentleman at her side had a kind face. He winked at me, this, no doubt, to smooth over what had just occurred. I supposed no affectionate conversations were to be taking place betwixt us. This suited me.

"Count Harold Davis and Lady Betina Davis; Lady Isabella Davis, of Cambridge, and Lady Katherine Thurgood, of Somerset," the man at the entryway to the ballroom announced

160

in an official, bored manner. I was learning that to look bored was fashionable. I hadn't known Aunt Betina married a count.

We bowed, curtseyed, and made our way to the edge of the room. There were chairs set about the perimeter of the room. Almost immediately, the family began conversing with those around them, and these were significant people to be sure. Barons, baronesses, magnates, earls; I suspected a large array of old wealth.

Already Isabella's dance card was filling up. I was unsure of what to do with myself, but soon I learned to join into any conversation she was having. As much as I felt I did not belong, no one need suspect it. A boy or two even asked the privilege of a dance with me. I was so giddy I could barely relinquish my book so that they may sign their names.

"Where is the Duke of Berkshire?" I whispered to Isabella.

"He will arrive later. You shan't be able to miss his entrance."

The music began to play, and the dance floor filled up two by two. The first man I danced with was an excellent dancer. I coached myself on the steps, head titled, back erect, smile on face. I can say it was rather more pleasant than I had imagined it could be. The sensation of being on the floor amidst all the swooshing gowns was indescribable. Perhaps this was the essence of joy itself.

I danced with the second young man, who was quite handsome, and while I had not another name in my book after that dance, I sat and observed Isabella and the others. This is when I met Thomas Remington. He walked over to me to request a dance, and as he extended his hand to assist me, I felt his touch was genuine. Should this be the one? As we danced I looked him over out of the corner of my eye. He appeared solid enough, genteel.

As the dance ended I made my decision. He didn't know it yet, but he was to be mine. It was against my nature to work over a person, but I feared for my survival. He linked his arm with mine to escort me over to the chairs, and I felt a strange bubbling sensation at the bottom of my stomach. I tried to think of something clever to say.

At that moment trumpets sounded and the ballroom went quiet. Everyone turned simultaneously. The Duke was fit to enter at any moment. I watched with great anticipation. Thomas was at my side still; it was my plan to retain him as long as I could.

The announcer spoke: "Presenting, His Grace, the Duke of Berkshire." We were a good distance away and my desire was to get a better look, but instead of moving forward I followed procedure, bowing and curtseying at his entrance. Now was my chance to get a look. As he made his way forward, the ballroom divided.

I blinked repeatedly. Surely there was something wrong with my eyes. I watched as the Duke pulled from the crowd what I could only assume was his lady, and when the music commenced again they led the ballroom in a dance.

"Are you well, Miss Thurgood?" Thomas asked. I imagine my face was as white as chalk. Mother would never believe this!

"Yes," I assured him as I blotted my brow with my kerchief. "Dance with me," I ordered, aware I was breaking with convention.

"Pardon me?" he asked in complete bewilderment.

"Please—you don't ever have to dance with me again," I urged, and positioned myself for the dance. He obliged me. My only quest in life was now to avoid being seen by the Duke. Appearing pleasant was proving more difficult. As far as I could see from my periphery, we were not near to the Duke and his lady. When the dance had ended Thomas again escorted me back to where he had first met me.

"I thank you so, Mr. Remington. Please forgive me if I was too forward."

"The pleasure was mine. If you don't mind, I would be pleased to call upon you sometime. Where may I find you?"

I averted my eyes. "I will be at Holmsbridge, Lady Braithwaite's home in Somerset, for only another week or so."

"Perhaps you will see me there?" he asked with a smile. I curtseyed, and blushed as he disappeared into the crowd.

"Ooh, he *is* delicious!" Isabella exclaimed to me once he was out of earshot. "Come," she said and pulled me along.

"I can't," I said when I saw the general direction we were headed.

"Don't be silly. Nana made it clear to us we were to make an impression for the family. Mother and Father intend to meet His Grace."

"But I cannot, I am not supposed to be known as a member of the family."

"You can't think I would let you miss this? You are my special guest, remember?"

What could I do? I was not permitted to cross the ballroom or leave the ballroom without an escort.

We waited in line for a few minutes before the Duke was free to speak with Isabella's parents. I did well to keep myself hidden. As we neared, it was impossible to deny that the visage before me was the one and only Mr. Roeing, though this name had obviously been an alias. Was this the reason Mrs. Dunham had winked at him when she'd said his name back in Chatworthy House?

Roeing Oaks indeed!

As my family stood before him I kept myself off to the side. No one bothered to introduce me in any case. Surely he saw me, and did well to pretend that he did not. My heart beat at an impossible speed as I listened to him converse with them. Suddenly I felt indecent, with so much skin exposed at my décolletage. My hand was drawn magnetically to my collarbone.

"Is this young lady in your party?" he asked, turning his head to look at me. I coughed in spite of myself. "My, what an exquisite hairpiece!" he commented.

"Forgive me, Your Grace, I was about to introduce her to you. This is my dear friend Miss Katherine Thurgood," Isabella said. As I turned my head, courage entered me. I looked him directly in the eye, daring him to call me out. I curtseyed.

"Your Grace," I greeted.

"A pleasure," he said, and bowed. "Miss Thurgood, where does one acquire such a piece as you sport in your hair?" I could see my aunt was displeased at the attention I was receiving. I cleared my throat.

"This piece was—please, forgive my unstable memory. I cannot recall from whence it came, Your Grace. I have seen others like it. I've considered it a possible piece of costume jewelry."

"Surely it isn't Katherine, it's a wonderful piece," said Isabella. "Oh! Your employer. Did you not tell me it was from your employer?" she suggested cheerfully. Her face then soured as she realized the mistake she had made in making me appear

165

to be part of the working classes. I laughed nonchalantly. She joined in.

"Don't be silly, Isabella. As it turns out, I do recall who gave it to me. It was only a silly boy from home who once took a faint interest in me."

"I declare, the interest could not have been faint," he said, looking me directly in the eye. I hoped no one could see my skin flushing. Then, as smooth as still water, he turned the conversation. "Have you met Lady Bristol?" he asked us collectively.

"No, Your Grace, we have not had the most distinct honour of doing so. She is the loveliest in the kingdom, isn't that right, Harold?" gushed my aunt as she nudged her husband.

If the Duke sensed her false enthusiasm, he did not let on. We were led directly to the lovely subject. Being face to face with Lady Bristol confirmed my worst fears. She truly was the loveliest in the kingdom. Even Isabella paled in comparison. And poor Isabella—she was unaccustomed to being humbled and did not know how to react.

Lady Bristol's eyes were large and dark—other worldly—and her complexion was pale and glowing, as a cherub. Her chestnut hair was of perfect sheen and thickness, and was piled on her crown with the greatest skill, intertwined with ribbons and rare flowers. She was a virtual Athena.

"How do you do?" we all greeted. Lady Bristol merely nodded her head in a manner I imagined the Queen would, when showing mercy to her subjects.

"It has been our pleasure to have made your acquaintance," the Duke said with a smile. He stood beside her, a worthy counterpart. "Do enjoy the banquet, and the dancing. There are many lovely trivialities to partake in this evening."

This was how the Duke dismissed us.

Chapter Eighteen

I paced the chamber, my mind in a frenzy. Was I meant to go to sleep under the circumstances? I replayed the night in my mind and could make no sense of it.

At the banquet that followed our meeting with Mr. Roeing, we had been seated at a table that was near enough to the head table that I could study the Duke and his lady. From time to time his eyes would meet mine, but only for an instant, and I thought I read in them kindness. Or perhaps he was not meeting my eyes at all, and I was seeing a mirage like I had read about in a book from my grandfather's library.

In Hazel Grove I had informed Mr. Roeing I would be visiting my grandmother. Now I wondered what he thought of seeing me there with a wealthy family. Would he call me a liar? I could call him the same.

And Thomas, Thomas Remington, the dear boy who I had danced with, he studied me as well, searching for any intentions I suppose. I decided that I would still do what I could to steal his heart. After all, the mere impossibility that I had any chance of romance with the Duke, as my heart attempted to convince me, told me that winning over Thomas was a better option. As wonderful as Mr. Roeing had been to Mother and I, it had been another time and place. I could not expect assistance from him.

The remainder of the evening I focused away from Mr. Roeing as much as possible, channeling my passions to the young man Thomas, and all the while deflecting the insolent gaze of Aunt Betina. During my last dance with Thomas I asked if he knew the Duke personally. His father did, he'd said. He was going to announce his choice for marriage the following May; the Lady Bristol being the obvious guess.

And then all at once I found myself there in a bedchamber. An invitation had been given to my aunt and uncle to spend the evening at the castle and enjoy breakfast at the Duke's table the following morning. A room had been set aside for them. Assuming the invitation included myself, I followed along.

"No! How could you think the invitation extended to you? You are a bastard child! I'll tell His Grace first thing. He

169

wouldn't have such a miserly imp cross the threshold of his home!" said my dear aunt.

"Miss Katherine Thurgood?" asked an attendant. I looked from my aunt and back to the attendant.

"Yes?"

"Please follow me. Your room is this way." I looked in bewilderment at Isabella and her parents and turned to follow the attendant to a room several doors down. I would later cherish the outrage I had read on Aunt Betina's face.

I simply did not know what to do with myself when I reached the room. Somehow my traveling bag had made its way into my room. After inspecting it, I paced until I was exhausted, and finally came to a decision.

I knew that I could fall into grave trouble, but I did not in that moment care a mite. I went to the door. I would find this duke and speak with him, if it meant being expelled from the kingdom. Just as I grasped the door knob it seemed to turn of its own accord. I gasped.

"Miss Thurgood," said the same attendant that had escorted me there not long before.

"Yes, sir."

"His Grace will see you now."

I stopped trying to make sense of it all and followed behind him as he rounded the corner. Not fifty paces away the attendant knocked on a great mahogany door.

"Enter," I heard Mr. Roeing say from behind the door. When the door was pushed open I saw him behind the great mahogany desk, his feet propped casually atop it, his hands folded across his midsection. He had a curious expression on his face, something like a smirk.

The new me vanished, and I was again Kate from Hazel Grove: the poverty stricken, deprived soul of which nothing was expected save swiftness of service. I retreated into myself.

"Bring her forth," he instructed the attendant.

The attendant motioned I come forward. We stopped dangerously near to the desk. Once he had stepped back, I curtseyed to Mr. Roeing. Without removing his eyes from me, he dismissed the attendant. I could not seem to raise my head again under the thickness of the air. After the door was securely closed, it seemed an eternity before a word was uttered. I heard the sound of feet dismounting and settling on the floor.

"How fare you, Miss Thurgood? I trust you are quite well. I knew you would not find rest until we had spoken."

How casual a greeting.

"I am well, and pleased to be in your company; thank you, your grace," I answered, raising my eyes just enough make contact. I saw him smile faintly before I lowered my eyes again.

171

He stood and leaned over the desk, clasping my hands. "Please, sit," he said, nodding to a chair off the desk's corner. Then he squeezed my hands and let them go.

"Thank you, Your Grace," I replied, and took the seat. I did my best to appear unshaken as he also sat.

"It's lovely to see you again," he said. My heart shrunk within me. I had tried so hard to forget his warmth. "How is your grandmother?"

"W-well. It is almost time for me to return to Hazel Grove. I am afraid she has had her fill of me."

"Is that possible, Kate?" he asked with a laugh. Was he flirting? Absurd!

I cleared my throat. "Have you heard from Mother?" I wished to know if he had heard of my fate as well.

"No, I have not. She is well, I hope? And Joseph?"

"Yes, certainly." Was I to tell him, or should I save him the burden? After a moment of silence I asked him the question. "May I ask why His Grace has brought me here tonight?"

"Are you quite disappointed with me?" he asked with a solemn expression.

"In what way Your Grace?"

He held out his hand. "Please, you needn't address me so."

"Would you have me address you as Mr. Roeing, even though we both know that is not your name?" I turned my head away. "Forgive me if I have been too bold with you," I added for good measure.

"Would you feel more comfortable to know that my true name is Edward Oakes? I'm afraid Roeing Oaks is a bit of a play on words. Roeing was my great-grandfather's Christian name, and the oaks are, well, styled after our surname," he added with a smile. "The old man hated the name Grimsby Hall, so he replaced it with Roeing Oaks."

Edward Oakes. So droll.

"It may have been helpful to have known your identity all along. I'm afraid I've misjudged you."

"Do not be dismayed. Anonymity can be a great gift, and at times I choose to walk in it." He paused, studied my expression. "You look beautiful tonight. Not a resemblance to the quaint girl I left in Hazel Grove. They have groomed you well. When I first saw I confess my breath left me."

"If that is so then why did you pretend you did not know me?"

"You know why. How should I explain to your family? Anyway they needn't be concerned with my doings in Hazel Grove."

"My family? I have come as a guest of the Braithwaites," I said, to test his wits.

"Is that what they call you? A guest?" He clucked his tongue and shifted his weight so that he was leaning forward.

173

"Do you remember the evening before you left, the conversation we had?"

My stomach leapt at the recollection of my feelings in that moment. "Yes," I whispered.

"We talked of secrets. And mine was of a certain man with a furtive past, whose secret I had discovered—a man of high rank in society who had sold his wife so that he could go on to marry his lover. He told his wife's family how she had run away with a mysterious lover, and the result was that she was disavowed from her family. Oh, yes, and she was pregnant with his child."

A tear ran down my cheek. He stood and came before me. "I couldn't let it go. I had to find this woman and this child, see what had become of them. I didn't expect to find—" he trailed off.

I stood before him. "Why? Why have you brought me here? Now that you know the end of the story, what is it to you?"

"Who are you really, Kate? Are you the girl from Hazel Grove, the milkmaid's daughter, the maid-of-all-work, or are you Katherine, the strong, privileged, cultured young lady?"

"I don't suppose I know the answer. Is there a choice to be made? And you? Who are you?"

"What do you need me to be?" he asked gently. He shook his head as if to forget what he'd just uttered. "Come," he said as he linked elbows with me and escorted me to the door. I leaned into him.

"There is much to think on. You need to rest. It has been such a pleasure to be in your presence again. I can only hope it has been a marvelous evening for you."

"Yes, of course. It is always wonderful to be—to see you. Will Lady Bristol be in attendance at breakfast?" I asked, sinking a bit at the thought.

"Yes." He bowed his head and raised it again. "All is well. Do rest well." He grasped my head in his hands and gently kissed my forehead. "Please understand I cannot escort you back to your room. Do you recall the way?"

I nodded again, and smiled sheepishly. I thought of one last question.

"Sir, wherever did you get such a piece as I am wearing in my hair now?"

"It is a family heirloom." He winked at me, or so it seemed.

I looked up into his eyes, and not understanding my own words said, "I trust you, sir. I do." He gave my hands a squeeze and ushered me out the door.

I turned and walked down the hall, giddy with all that had happened. When at my own door I turned the knob to find quite a surprise. It was Isabella, sitting on the chaise. I nearly screamed.

"What are you doing here?"

"I might ask where you have been! Mother has decided our suite was too small for the three of us. I have been instructed to share with you." Were those tear stains on her cheek?

"Have you been crying?" I asked, approaching her.

"It's nothing. Mother always puts me in a sour mood. Now where have you been?"

"Can you keep a secret?" I asked.

She leaned forward. "Yes, of course!"

"Good, I wondered about that," I teased.   Isabella pouted.

"Oh, I was only exploring the manor!"

"That is all? No secret love affairs? You know you could get into a lot of trouble for roaming around this place." If only she knew. "Don't you find the Duke stunning?" she asked.

"I don't know if I would say stunning. There is something about him."

As I lay in bed, sleep avoided me. Was that all Mr. Roeing wanted from me? To know the end of the story? I could not wait to behold him at the breakfast table.

Chapter Nineteen

Breakfast did not fare as I expected. The dining hall was massive, and the guests many. Our seat was nearly the length of the vast table away from Mr. Roeing and Lady Bristol. I spent the duration craning my ear to hear anything he said, while intently studying the interaction between them.

Meanwhile, I had Aunt Betina to stave off and another eye on Mr. Thomas Remington, whose family was also in attendance. He smiled at me often. Was I to smile in return or was that vulgar? What if Mr. Roeing saw this interaction and assumed we were a pair? Was he looking at all? He did have such a keen eye. If I did not smile in return, would Thomas still come to call on me at Holmsbridge? I found myself longing for it all to be over, and before long it was.

With a curtsey to the Duke and his lady as I passed through the receiving line before the door, it was all over. I was left to wonder what it was all about, and still what I would do next, as I knew I could not return to Hazel Grove. Why hadn't I arranged a way to contact Mr. Roeing when I had the chance? Now I would not know when we could speak again. I should at least have thought to ask if he would be returning to Hazel Grove.

The following day at Holmsbridge, Isabella and I remained largely silent as we thought on the events that passed, save at meal times when the Madam interrogated us about every detail of our time at Roeing Oaks.

As we sat in the drawing room after tea, I pretending to read a book, and Isabella practicing at the piano, Reginald appeared.

"A message for you, Miss Thurgood." He handed me a note and was gone before I could thank him. I broke the wax seal immediately.

"It's from Thomas Remington!" I squealed. "He wants to come calling! Oh, how do I give him permission? Do I write him a reply?" I asked.

"You little devil! You must first ask Nana's permission. I don't see why she would mind. Come, let us inquire," she said and we giggled on our way to find the Madam. As we passed near the entryway, we looked out the window and noticed a man on horseback coming down the lane and decided to spy who it might be.

"It's Jonathan! Quickly, answer the door before the footmen see!" Isabella cried.

"Well, did he say he was coming to call?" I whispered.

"No, of course not!" We hurried toward the entryway.

We ran outside toward the stables in the chilly afternoon air and motioned him toward us. We dismissed the stable boy and awaited Jonathan inside the stables. Once the horse was secured he came our way. I hoped he wouldn't find the situation odd. His countenance was strained, and he was breathless.

Isabella spoke first, her tone sympathetic. "Whatever is the matter, dear Jonathan? Are you vexed?" He looked over at me.

"I've come to see *her*. I must speak with her alone." Isabella and I looked at one another, she with jealousy and I with contempt. If she had been obedient and stayed away from him this would not have been happening. I braced myself for the interrogation that was sure to follow.

"Isabella, you must await me indoors," I said matter-of-factly. She opened her mouth to protest, then thought better of it and bid Jonathan good-day. She looked over her shoulder until she disappeared around the corner.

"Mr. Percy, you cannot come here without first calling." I walked further in the stables, hoping the air would be warmer within. He followed behind, looking up into the rafters to see if any of the stable hands were there.

179

"I had an interesting conversation last evening with my father," he said sharply. "Are you ready to speak of her?"

"Speak of whom?" I asked. I had turned around so that we were face to face.

"Victoria."

I laughed in disbelief. I didn't think my situation could get any worse. "First tell me of this interesting conversation with your father. How is the old bloke?" I hadn't known I could be so tongue in cheek, but Jonathan seemed to draw it out of me.

"I asked Father who Victoria was. I told him I had met someone who knew her. I can't say I recall seeing him lose his senses in quite such a way. It was worse than the first time back in spring. There was this fear in his eyes—and then rage. He was trembling. He wanted to know with whom I spoke and what I knew of her. I told him I had only heard it in passing, that the individual was a stranger to me." There was genuine concern in Jonathan's eyes. "You mustn't keep it from me any longer."

I blinked back my tears, looking up at the wooden ceiling beams. I knew I must say it and brave whatever consequence might overtake me. I would handle it somehow. I leaned against a pole and said it.

"Victoria is my mother. She is Lady Braithwaite's daughter."

"I thought she married Count—?"

"No, that is my aunt. Victoria is the firstborn and she has since been banished from the family and all of society because of what your father did."

"My father? My father is a good man."

"I can't say if he is or isn't. I only know the truth." From behind me the Madam's stallion snorted in his stall. "Your father was once married to her, to my mother."

"That's preposterous!"

I explained the story. "It's God's honest truth! He sold her to do away with the marriage quickly so that he could marry your mother. Apparently she was pregnant as well, and he wanted it all to be her! He wanted it to be her and you in his life!"

After some time in stunned silence, he laughed. "She's lying! My father would never do such a thing. What kind of woman is she to make up lies? A bitch, I'd say."

I felt as though I had been slapped. I stepped closer to him.

"It's true! Go on, confront him! He told the Braithwaites she had run off with another man and went to God-forsaken Australia of all places. They never spoke with her again until this past March. Anyway, doesn't that make *you* the bastard child? I am not the illegitimate one." I walked off in a fury.

181

He chased me down and took hold of my arm. I wriggled it loose. He caught hold of me again and thrust me against a pole.

"You had better not be lying to me. Do you mean to purport that you are my sister? That my father is your father?"

I looked down. I didn't wish to answer anymore questions. I felt him searching my face. I knew he was searching for a resemblance. His grip loosened and I felt his finger sweep over the mole above my left eyebrow, the mole we both had. He let go of me and paced the stable with one hand over his eyes. The silence was deafening.

"Does he know about you?" Jonathan asked quietly without looking at me.

"Yes," I answered.

"Has he seen you?"

"Only briefly."

"So this is what all the whispering has been about. The servants, lately they're always whispering. What am I to do with this information? And what are you doing here?"

"I wish I knew. My grandmother asked that I join her for the holidays. I do not know what her motive is. I know nothing anymore."

He pulled me to him. "You're coming with me."

Chapter Twenty

Jonathan literally dragged me kicking and screaming onto his horse. I feared I was being kidnapped. At last he shook me by the shoulders and assured me no harm would come to me. Somehow I was able to calm myself. He wrapped me in the cleanest horse blanket he could find in the stable to give me warmth and hopped in front of me onto the horse. I held to him tightly as we galloped to Longhurst. Soon after, Jonathan burst through the study doors of Alistair Percy with me in tow.

"Forgive me, Father, for the interruption, but I have something urgent to speak with you about." Alistair Percy appeared slightly jolted, but was otherwise in a controlled state of mind. I wondered how he would react to what was coming.

"I would like you to meet my friend, Miss Katherine Thurgood." Alistair looked me over and stood to bow.

"How do you do, Miss Thurgood?" he greeted, his eyes still upon me. I quickly curtseyed, then looked to Jonathan.

"Father, Miss Thurgood has a most interesting story, I'm sure you'll be delighted to learn it."

"Jonathan!" I whispered. He looked at me with insistence.

"You see, Thurgood is a sort of borrowed name, an adoptive name if you will."

"Son, I'm sure I *would* be delighted to hear the details but I'm afraid you're being conspicuous, and I have much to attend to at the moment."

"I understand, Father, but there is something—"

"Jonathan," Alistair said with a grumble, "this really isn't the time."

"Father, you never told me I had a sister!"

The room fell silent. I think even my heart stopped for fear that movement would upset Alistair. My breath left me as he walked slowly, deliberately, in my direction.

"I assure you, it's all lies, and the creator of such lies will pay. I will not have my family broken apart by heartless, greedy wenches."

Trepidation wrapped itself about me in that moment, constricting me until I thought I would faint. He stopped so close to me that I could smell his breath; cigars and gin.

"I have no children but this son, whose mother passed long ago, bless her soul. Take yourself and your intentions back to wherever it is you come from." I would rather have been spit on and had my wrists slit for me than to have heard that.

"Son, this is an imposter, a viper seeking her prey. Take her out of my sight! We will not speak of this again. And if I should find that you speak with her or any of the Braithwaites, your status as the family heir will be in jeopardy." He had more to say, but a fit of coughing overtook his ability to speak.

"Yes, Father," Jonathan said with his head bowed. He looked to me , and I understood it was time to make our exit. Suddenly I had courage enough to shoot a look of contempt at the man who spilled his seed into my mother's womb, only to mash it with the heel of his foot when it was brought forth.

"Why have you done this to me? Did I ask to be humiliated?" I demanded when we were outside. Jonathan kept walking toward the stables. I followed after.

"Will you ignore me? Will you not at least apologize for the way I was treated?" He held his hand out to me to help me mount the horse. I refused it until he would speak to me.

"It isn't my doing. It isn't either of our doing. There is nothing that can be done," he said with a blank expression. I felt he could at least look me in the eye.

"What now? Do we part ways, never to speak again? Is that all?"

185

"His expectations of me are high; they always have been. I cannot risk my future over this."

"Your future? You don't honestly think he would do that do you? Strip you of your inheritance? Is he so evil?"

Jonathan snapped his head up. "You don't know him to accuse him so! He isn't evil!"

"He looked me in the face and denied me!" I threw my hands up in the air and circled the horse.

"Do you know what happens to me, my future? In one week I am to leave Holmsbridge. If all were well I would return to our hamlet in Hazel Grove, and at best I would live out my days as a farm labourer, a milkmaid. Mr. Boyle, our landlord, would continue to rob us of wages and treat Mother and I as pigs. That is if all were well. But it isn't well, Jonathan. When our landlord discovered I had gone to stay with my grandmother he was livid. I am no longer welcome to return. As it is, I do not know what I will do, where I will go. I can't tell my grandmother; she already sees me as lowly. This is my inheritance."

"I'm assuming my father obtained a legal divorce after—the incident?" he asked me.

"Well, yes, that's what I've heard. Why?"

"Katherine, you can't dispute this. By law you are illegitimate because your parents were divorced at the hour of your birth. Did you know that?" I shook my head no. "You cannot just waltz in here and expect to be one of us. If he did it, I'm sorry—but am I in a position to—to help? And anyway, why should I? Do I even know you?" he cried, running his fingers through his hair.

"Help me onto the horse," I insisted, but he did not move. "I said help me on the damn horse!" It was the first time I recalled ever having used profanity. Jonathan held out his hand.

"Perhaps you shouldn't. If he sees you on my horse he'll—"

"Would you have me to find my own way in the dark? What is the matter with all of you? You brought me here! I didn't ask for it, I didn't ask!" I began to sob, to beat the side of the saddle with my fists.

Jonathan climbed onto the horse. We rode in silence. The icy wind sliced at my wetted face as a razorblade. When we arrived, he calmly told me it was best he did not escort me to the door. I knew it was best, yet I longed for him to stand before the Madam by my side as a fortress, to fight for me— nevertheless I was left alone.

I arrived to dinner just as dessert was being served. My clothing was rumpled, and I am sure my countenance was gray and my hair in awful disarray. I did not make an effort to fix myself.

The Madam's manner was cold that night. I apologized for my tardiness. I should have thought that my puffy, red eyes might have been cause to inquire if something was amiss, yet no word was spoken. I seated myself.

"If you would have your dinner you must eat below stairs with the servants. Dessert is arriving and I can't bear to watch you eat meat during our sweets," the Madam said without looking up.

"Thank you, but dessert will suffice," I said as I glanced at Isabella, who did not look up from her plate. I realized she had not covered for me. Was she so jealous I had Jonathan's attention that she tattled on me? As dessert was placed before me I tested the waters.

"Grandmother," I began, knowing well it would frazzle her to be addressed so, "I declare, winter is surely upon us. I have just returned from an extended stroll and I found the wind to be markedly wicked."

She shuddered. "Is it then?" she answered as politely as she could. She dabbed her napkin on her chin.

"Yes, in fact I believe I sense a storm coming from the north, not far from, say, Longhurst. I feel it could be headed our direction. I only ask, if such a front hits Holmsbridge, what will you do to fortify?"

The Madam dropped her fork onto her plate. She turned to face me. "Do you mean to be coy with me? I can only answer that it would be lucky, nay, timely, for the storm to curb in the direction of your train as you take it home!"

"Oh, it most certainly will curb in that direction. But at times a storm leaves a trail which can be quite destructive. Mother knows this all too well."

"Do you dare accuse me of some sort of wrongdoing?" the Madam answered, her anger boiling like a pot of stew over the fire.

"Certainly not. I am sure your benevolent nature will prompt you to abet her, or to beseech Aunt Betina to do so."

"We don't need such controversy."

Ooh! I scolded myself for ever wishing to be one of them! I looked over at Isabella. Could she say nothing on my behalf? Would she truly sit and allow me to suffer? She would, and she sat pushing her dessert around on her plate with a fork. I thought perhaps I should tell them that I had nowhere to go, but I realized this would only strain the situation further. I stood.

"You're all the same," I said under my breath. I fought back my tears and as I walked from the room.

In the Blue Room I paced. What was the next step? I had never been adept at taking control of things, or at planning. Come morning, I knew one thing: I must be gone. It would be ungainly for all for me to stay on a few more days. I penned a letter to Mother, assuring her I had worked something out and would write again soon.

Next, Mr. Thomas Remington. Now there would be no chance with him. I penned him a reply stating that while I was flattered at his interest in calling, I must rush home to attend to a family matter and would not be available for him to call for some time. I ended that I had quite enjoyed our time together at Roeing Oaks.

Mr. Roeing, His Grace the Duke of Berkshire, Edward Oakes...how I longed to speak with him! I imagined myself back in Hazel Grove, swinging under the oak tree in my youth. Would I never swing on it again?

I found my old carpetbag and began to pack my belongings. What was mine? I had arrived with a faded calico dress and not much more. I could not find the calico and did not wish to take the clothes afforded me by the Madam. In the end I would need to take them; I had nothing else. I prayed that it wasn't stealing and told myself I would repay the Madam one day for what I took. I picked out the two most sensible dresses I could find; one I placed in the trunk, and the other I changed into. I could not imagine I would need anything fancy. What I would need was employment of some sort.

After I had finished packing, being careful not to forget the hairpiece from Mr. Roeing, I sat on the bed to collect myself. Glancing over at the bookshelf, a black book with gold lettering caught my eye. The Holy Bible. Why hadn't I noticed it before? I got up and took it off the shelf. It seemed far too sacrilegious to take a Bible so I simply paged through it, searching for something, I didn't know what. My eye fell on words that seemed to glow on the page.

"And they shall fight against thee, but they shall not prevail against thee; for I am with thee, says the Lord, to deliver thee." (Jeremiah 1:19).

It seemed another was in the room with me, and I was imbued with a warm wave of assurance, as I'd felt in the forest when I desired to escape Ethan and somehow found strength. I turned my head carefully to be sure that I was, as I thought, alone. I breathed a sigh of relief and replaced the book on the shelf.

Moments later I was out the door, my carpetbag in tow and a stolen lantern in hand. My exit from Holmsbridge had gone unnoticed.

Chapter Twenty-one

I took my chances that Alistair Percy would be a safe distance away when I knocked on Longhurst's door. I did not know what I would do if I came face to face with him again. The butler answered.

I asked for Jonathan, instructing him that I would await him outside. Strange he did not ask my name or to state my business. I left my lantern on the lowest step and hid in the shadows, wondering if I had alerted the butler of some mischief, or worse, if he had gone on to tell Alistair of my presence. If trouble came I would have to flee. I did not know the lay of the land and would not know in which direction to run.

I exhaled when I saw Jonathan appear in the doorway. He paused to scope his surroundings, then walked tentatively down the steps.

"Jonathan! I'm over here," I whispered. I'd startled him. As was becoming his custom with me, he took hold of my elbow, and escorted me further into the darkness.

"Do you not understand, girl, how dangerous it is for you to be here?" he said through gritted teeth. "He would have both our heads!"

"Let go of me! You really don't know your own strength, you beast!" I said, genuinely angered. "I had no choice. I've been run off! They knew I was with you. Surely you don't think I would endanger either of us without just cause!"

"I don't know what to think of you!" He kicked at a stone.

"Listen, it pains me to ask, but I've nowhere to go and only a few pence. Might I borrow enough money—for a train ticket at least? I don't know where I'll go but I can't stay around here. I could pay you back as soon as I make some money; and you'll never have to speak with me again. I'll be gone forever, I promise!"

He bowed his head. "You're being truthful with me now? You aren't conning me out of money? This whole—story isn't some scheme?" he asked.

"Surely not," I insisted. Were his heartstrings unattainable like all the rest?

"All right," he conceded. "We'll have to wait until he's asleep. Stay here. It may take a while, but I'll be back."

"But I—"

Jonathan had gone. I was left to wonder if he would truly come back, or if it was a trap. I felt I had no other choice but to wait. I sat down and leaned up against the manor. The sounds of night were frightening: creatures stirring, owls cooing. Holding my bag close to me, I relaxed myself as best I could considering the winter winds. Probably from the exhaustion of fear, I fell asleep.

I started with a gasp when I felt my arm being nudged. It was Jonathan.

"Come," he said, putting his finger to his mouth.

I followed him into the stables. After several minutes, he led his saddled horse to the entrance. Then he bent down on one knee to provide me with a stool to mount the horse

"You'd best not attempt to ride side saddle. We will go through rough terrain." I reluctantly straddled the horse. He climbed on in front of me. "Hold on," he said.

In a way I felt I was being rescued, and I was grateful, yet I did not know where he was taking me, or why. It could still go quite badly. I put my arms around his waist and held on as we galloped away into the darkness. It felt natural to be so near to him.

Luckily the moon was full so that our path was dimly lit. In about a quarter of an hour's ride we arrived at a small hunter's cabin. Jonathan helped me dismount the horse and led me indoors. He set about kindling a fire with what little wood was stacked beside the fireplace.

I looked 'round. It was sparse and masculine; outside of that, it was reminiscent of our cottage back home. There were four bunks against the back wall, a table with four chairs, a bookshelf, a couple of braided rugs atop a roughly planked floor. Everything was under cover.

"Father doesn't prefer to hunt past November. He detests the chill. He's had it closed until spring, so you should be safe here. The chimney smoke shouldn't alert anyone, either. There are a dozen other cabins throughout the forest." He began uncovering a bed and the table.

"And in the morning?" I asked.

"In the morning I shall bring you some food."

"I am much obliged, but what of the train ticket? I would be delighted if you would only help me obtain one."

Jonathan smiled, but the smile was one of mockery. "A train ticket to where? Shall I set you about to wander the earth? You must stay here until we figure what to do with you."

"We? Do you intend to assist me?" I asked with a laugh. His smile faded.

"Do you have better options? As I said, I will return in the morning with foodstuffs. You do know how to prepare meals?"

"Do you ask this of a farm girl?" I asked, looking around at my new quarters.

"Yes, of course. I had forgotten. And one of those? Do you know how to use one of those?" he asked, pointing at the rifles mounted on the wall.

"I'm a rather good shot, actually."

"Good, then you ought to be well-suited to staying here. I bid you goodnight."

With the closing of the door, I was alone for the evening. So this is what it had come to. I entertained the idea that this could still all be a trap, but inside I knew it was not. I tried not to feel frightened. I slept that night with a loaded rifle by my side.

Jonathan arrived in the morning with the promised provisions. He scolded me for keeping the rifle so close by. After an awkward time in which he disappeared and reappeared with more kindling, he left again.

What a puzzle he was.

The third day was officially Christmas, and I passed it alone, save for the few moments Jonathan sneaked away from his holiday doings to bring me a plate of delicious food. I thought mostly of Mother, Joseph, and yes, my dear Mr. Roeing. I imagined us happily dressing a tree and sitting down to a lovely meal, perhaps even exchanging gifts. What gift would I give to Mr. Roeing?

I would see Jonathan sporadically over the next week. He dropped by with more provisions, a few days later to check on my well-being, again with more provisions. Our communications were always clipped and reserved. Always he darted off before I could invite him to stay and take tea with me. He seemed unsure whether he wished to know me, or if he should help me to move on.

I was growing lonely. The silence was becoming maddening and I craved human contact. I took turns being content, then discontent, hopeful, then hopeless. There was no measure to time or circumstance. I began to talk to myself, then to God. And strangely, it seemed I heard him answer back. Not hearing in the physical sense, but words; or if not words, thoughts, ideas. I found myself obsessing over unwarranted desires.

I began to discover that in my being laid desires to do things, important things. Escaping poverty so that I could see the world, make some kind of difference, this was the main thing. It was an itch that could not be reached to scratch. During the day I would hike through the general area to get these things off my mind or go to the pond nearby to fish. I napped more than anything, and read what literature Jonathan brought for me to read.

It was now the first day of the New Year. I made a steamed pudding in celebration, for I knew Jonathan would be dropping in to see me. I wanted to please him, and it was all I could offer. When he arrived, lo and behold, he came bearing a steamed pudding! We laughed about the coincidence. It was good to share a laugh with him.

At last I persuaded him to stay for tea. Not for long, but tea it was. I ventured to ask if he had thought on what to do next with me. He avoided answering by asking if there was anything I needed. He had given me every request. I could think of nothing more to ask for.

Suddenly he was ready to go.

"Jonathan, surely you can't keep me here for the rest of my life," I said.

He stopped, looked down. "I'm not sure I want you to go yet." Then he was gone.

I pouted and returned to my half-eaten pudding. I sat contemplating if I should finish it all, even though I knew it would make my stomach sick. It was a new year, after all, a time for indulgence. I put my head down on the table and moaned. A knock at the door caused me to jump up. Jonathan would not knock so heavily. I was sure it was not him by the second knock. I scurried to the gun rack.

"Kate? Kate, are you in there?"

I ran my hand over my hair to smooth it and hurried to open the door. My eyes were as wide as birth when they rested upon my dear Mr. Roeing. Without a thought I fell upon his neck. He laughed.

"My, such a warm welcome!" he said as he wrapped his arms around me. I felt complete in that instant, wonderful and complete. I let go and looked him in the face.

"Is it really you?" I asked, squeezing his cheeks. "How did you know where to find me? Come in! Why aren't you at—I have steamed pudding—"

He followed me in and explained that he'd followed Jonathan into the forest, or he would have never found me. I took his coat from him and led him to the small table, poured him a cup of tea, babbling on about nothing as I did. When we were seated I sighed and looked at him, and he at me. He was dressed in common clothes. Was it a disguise? Suddenly the uncertainty of why he had come crept all over me like an asp. Was he the bearer of some horrid news? How else would he have known my whereabouts? All the pleasure drained from my face.

"Mr. Roeing? Why have you come?"

"I've just come from Chatworthy House."

Chapter Twenty-two

Mr. Roeing produced a letter. "Here, this is from your mother."

I snatched it from his hand. "You must tell me! Is she ill? Is something the matter with her? Or Joseph? Why have you been to Chatworthy House?"

"Only for a visit at the holidays. I expected to encounter you there as well."

"How are they? Mother and Joseph—" He laughed.

"Read it and you shall see."

I opened the letter and scanned its contents, grabbing my heart in relief at what I read. All was well. Mother and Joseph were in good health, although they missed me as dearly as I did them. There was also news that a family would be hiring out the Chatworthy House in the spring, and again Mother's wages would inflate. I was so happy for her! I smiled at Mr. Roeing as I wiped a tear from my cheek.

"It was she who told you where to find me?" I asked him. She must have received the letter I penned from the cabin. Jonathan truly was trustworthy to deliver it.

"Yes. Why did you not notify me yourself?" Mr. Roeing asked.

"You? I can't pretend to imagine with all your business you should need yet another distraction."

"You know any distraction from you is no distraction at all, yes?" I flushed. He continued. "Need I ask all the details as to how you came here? I felt as though I were trespassing finding my way here."

"I thought you knew everything," I teased. "And you *were* trespassing. So am I. Oh, it's all so tangled! Even you couldn't fix it at this point. I live for the day when I will know what tomorrow holds. For now, I am here."

I didn't know how much information Mr. Roeing was privy to, and he did not press me further. A part of me wished he would.

"Well, enough of me. How is life? How is Lady Bristol?"

"She is well," he said, smiling. I had just left off with her before going to Chatworthy House.

"She is extraordinary. Such a beauty," I added.

"Yes, of course. When we met I knew she was something very special indeed." Mr. Roeing grabbed hold of my hand. I looked into his eyes questioningly. He smiled.

"Something has changed in you," he said.

I removed my hand to employ it at pouring more tea. "I can't say that anything is different. Do you mean that I appear conflicted? Because I am; I am quite conflicted."

"Tell me about this."

"Aside from the present dangers, I have these urges inside to, to—I'm not sure what, do things with myself. Go places. And how? How? How would I get to the place where I would have the means to do any of it?" I sighed. "I can't explain."

"Do you feel so strongly that you don't think you could ever return to how you were before?"

"Yes! Yes, that's exactly it."

"Then God is doing a work in you. His plans are going accordingly. Remember when I asked you who you were? You must first know it and believe it before it can come to pass."

I contemplated his words. "But these things within me, they're not ordinary. They're beyond what—well, they're impossibly grand."

"Is God a small God?" he asked. I smiled.

"What about you? What do you do with yourself when you aren't traipsing about masquerading as a farmer? I'm afraid you're a mystery to me."

"Well, I go about helping people, I suppose you could say. There is much that needs to change in our society. Children are sorely mistreated, especially in London. You wouldn't believe the condition of the poor there. I work with people who can do something with the law, enforce regulations. And there are people going around selling their spouses. It's quite a travesty," he said, winking.

I smiled at the pun. "How fascinating, sir. Truly, how fascinating, and beautiful!"

"Listen, Kate, I can't stay long. I have something, an invitation. Speaking of the Lady Bristol, I would be so much obliged if you would come to a ball; an engagement ball. In May I will be announcing publicly my bride-to-be."

"Yes, I've heard."

"Have you then? Well, I wouldn't have you miss it for the world, you and your mother. Half the kingdom will be there, I suppose, but it wouldn't mean a thing to me if the people that mean the most were absent. Please, say you'll come."

How could I deny him anything, with those eyes bearing into me as they were?

"I would be delighted to," I said, taking the invitation from his hand. His happiness was more important to me than my own. If the Lady Bristol was a contributor to his happiness, I would be her lifelong support—even if it meant the end of something beautiful for me.

He smiled once more. "I'm so happy." He kissed my hand. "I know you find yourself in a bit of a pinch, but know that with Jonathan you are in good hands. I'm afraid I have to leave you now. If you should need anything, send me notice at Roeing Oaks, yes?"

"But you've only just arrived!" I complained. Still, I helped him put his jacket back on.

"Sir, I just want you to know how happy I am for you and the Lady Bristol. It's wonderful that you found her."

He turned and looked at me. "Truly?" He sounded skeptical.

"Is it so shocking that I should be happy for you?"

He leaned over and kissed my forehead. "In May, then?" he asked as he pulled the door open. Was he now in some hurry? I imagined the Lady Bristol to be awaiting him somewhere in the forest, if not sitting delicately before the fire in one of the rooms at Roeing Oaks.

"Yes, certainly. May," I answered. I watched him until he was out of sight, and I was alone as before. I stood there at the door, numb to the sensation of cold, until a squirrel scampered by to bring my thoughts back to reality. I closed the door, walked to the table to sit by the hearth. May? That was several months away; such a long time to go without seeing him. And after, I may never see him again.

I ate vengefully until all the pudding was finished. Then I threw my fork across the room. Each time I tried to forget him, get over him, there he was again. What was it he wanted from me? What was it anyone wanted from me? I had nothing to give.

I jumped at the sound of knocking at the door.

"Kate!" called the voice as the person opened the door. It was only Jonathan. At any other time I would have been grateful to receive him. I hid the invitation.

"Kate, you must come with me." He was short of breath and his complexion was pale. How could he have grown so careworn in an hour's time since I'd seen him?

"What is it?" I asked.

"It's Father; his liver. The doctor fears he won't live much longer."

"What do you wish for me to do?"

Jonathan bit his lip. "I thought that you should be there."

I could see that my presence was desired more as a support for himself. I was flattered that he wished me to be

205

with him, yet I could not see having to face that awful man again.

"Jonathan, I—" I began. I shook my head.

"You could stay there at Longhurst, only until he—the doctor thinks it won't be more than a few days. He's been ignoring the pain for a long while; too long. I tried to tell him to get examined but he would not heed my advice."

"You saw how he treated me! And what will people say of my presence?"

"The servants know already, they whisper incessantly. If anyone comes you will hide away until they're gone. Please? It is the duty of the children to comfort their parents in these times."

I bit my tongue. *My* duty it was not. *Parent*? Did Jonathan even know the meaning of the term? Nevertheless I put my feelings aside.

"For you, Jonathan; I will do it for you."

Chapter Twenty-three

I shall never be able to banish from my senses the acrid scent of near-death. It was well after dusk when I at last allowed Jonathan to usher me into the room of our father. I had hoped that in waiting to do so I would find him asleep. My assumptions were correct.

I gasped as I looked him over. How long had he been suffering? Had I not left his presence only a couple of weeks before?

There he lay, a pitiful heap of waning flesh. No longer was his expression foreboding; if it was, the jaundice disguised it well. Already his face was beginning to hollow, and the two or more days of stubble gave him the appearance of a beggar, rather than a man of power. For half a moment I rejoiced to see him so after everything I experienced at his hand. I repented of it immediately. He was a human being and he deserved my mercy. I feared to come too near, lest I wake him.

"I did not expect to see him this way," I whispered to Jonathan.

I noticed a tear escaping his eye and I reached over to hold his hand. He recoiled at my touch. Rubbing his eyes, he took two paces from me.

"Keep vigil for me, will you? Just for tonight," he whispered. I peeked my head out into the corridor, not sure of what I was looking for.

"Why not a servant? I hardly think I am the one he wishes to wake to," I answered at last.

"I have not been sleeping, Katherine. I have kept vigil several nights already. Repay me for my kindness toward you, and keep watch," he pleaded.

"But a servant—better, a nurse—" I protested.

"No, no. You."

"I do not wish to appear ungrateful for your kindness, but you know well how he feels about me!"

"He won't know it's you. He's in and out of consciousness. All I ask is for you to come and fetch me if there are any problems. I will stay in the room adjacent."

I knew what problems he was speaking of: retching, moaning, or the hour of death.

My silence was taken as compliance, and I found myself sitting in the corner of the room, listening to staggered breathing, inhaling the same moist, dense air as the patient. In the beginning I could not look upon his face; it was too terrible a sight. The sound of the clock ticking in the background was the only anchor to reality.

Avoiding sleep proved to be no difficulty with the moaning, and with the fervor of my own thoughts. I wondered all manner of things about the sick man. Was he in pain? Could he hear as Jonathan and I spoke? Had he thought of me at all as he watched his son grow? And Mother? Could there be some resentment within him for all he caused us?

By the time the cock began to crow, I rallied all my bravery and walked up to the bed. *You're not so intimidating,* I thought. Still, despite it all, compassion welled up inside of me, if only for his condition. I dared speak.

"It is I, Katherine. I-I read a story once, about Joseph in the Bible. His brothers did something terrible to him, and caused him much suffering. But in the end he was the winner. He said, 'What you have meant for evil, God has meant for good,' and he forgave them. I can't help but think this situation to be compared with Joseph, and that somehow, someway, what you did to Mother and I will turn for good. You can't stop it." I paused as he stirred. When I thought it safe I continued, sweat gathering at the nape of my neck.

209

"And so, what you have done to us, as God has forgiven me of my own wickedness, I must forgive you. I shall always be scarred, and though you have not asked it of me, my forgiveness is yours now." A heaviness lifted from me. I sighed and wiped the tears from my eyes.

I yelped as I felt something brush against my thigh. Turning, I saw the yellowed face turned in my direction with half-opened eyes. A strange gurgling sound emitted out of his pursed lips. I scurried off in a fright to fetch Jonathan.

Our father lived only two days more, and in that time I could not bring myself to return to the room. When at last Jonathan came to meet me, he requested I assist him with preparing the body for the wake. While in general there were people that could be hired for this, Jonathan insisted in the name of his father's dignity that we handle it, so that his nakedness would not be uncovered in the eyes of a stranger.

The nursemaid had already bound a strip of cloth about his head to keep his jaw from opening, and had placed a coin on each eyelid to keep them sealed. The jaundice was still present. In silence, we stripped the body, covering the private parts with a cloth. Vigorously we washed the body with spiced soap. It was already beginning to stiffen with rigor mortis, and a few times we had to massage the limbs to keep them pliable until we had finished.

Yes, death is uglier than deceit.

After assisting with the trousers and the remaining attire, I allowed Jonathan to attend to his hair and shave his face. I stood in the corner listening to his sniffling, trying not to be an intruder in the intimate grief of my brother.

A man was invited by Jonathan to help move the body to the casket and set it in just the right position. After, he injected the body with a mixture of arsenic and water, which he explained would help the body to remain set and more natural in appearance. This he deemed "embalming." With the use of a nude-coloured powder and a soft brush to the face and hands, he achieved a worldly skin-tone.

And so it was finished.

I left the room as the servants brought in flower arrangements and set them carefully about the parlour. Already they had stopped the clocks and covered the mirrors in hopes that the spirit of the dead would not become trapped within them. As well they had donned their mourning clothes, making the entire manor a true haunt to behold. The wake was to take place the following morning. I knew I would not be welcome to attend it, given the circumstances of our family secret.

As a servant delivered dinner to my chamber, Jonathan made his entrance. He appeared no more alive than our father after the events of the past few days. He waited until the servant exited before speaking.

"I thank you for all your assistance. I don't know what I would have done without it."

He was doing it again, speaking to me as though I were one of his employees, or worse, his servant. I sensed the end of my welcome fast approaching.

"This is why you did not wish me to take leave. You were afraid to face this alone," I said quietly. I had hoped there were other, less selfish reasons. He did not answer. "And where do I go now?" I asked, attempting to cover the desperation in my voice.

"You cannot stay. There will be questions. I have made arrangements for you."

"Pray tell."

"Father asked something of me before he passed. He mentioned Victoria, your mother, and he requested that out of his estate she be sent a monthly pension until the day of her death."

"Why, that's wonderful Jonathan! Did he truly say it?" I stood and began to approach him. He held his hand out and made a step backwards.

"Calm yourself, it isn't much, barely anything, in fact."

"If you only knew, Jonathan, how she lives—anything would be a great blessing. I am so happy he came to that decision."

212

Jonathan's countenance was as stone. "She cannot tell a soul, and neither you. You shall never mention the Percys again. If you do..."

"You needn't threaten me! Do you not understand me by now? You treat me as though I were demanding to collect half of the Percy estate."

"Do not presume to think you could attain it if you tried," he said through clenched teeth.

I allowed the silence to plead on my behalf. Jonathan softened, dug into his pocket.

"We have a friend in London. I have made arrangements for you to be trained as an assistant shopkeeper. In London, as anywhere, it is difficult to find adequate wages, especially for someone such as yourself with no trade skills. Unless you wish to end up in some sweatshop or working as a scullery maid—or worse—I suggest you follow instructions. I trust you will not disappoint," he said. A warning.

He handed me a roll of bills and a paper. "You will leave in the morning. I have also arranged for you to stop at Leechman's and obtain two serviceable suits of clothes, as well as anything else you think you may need. I have an account there; no need to pay mind to the balance. Your train departs at ten o'clock, so you should have plenty of time."

Then, he issued the final blow.

213

"I shouldn't think you will have need of mourning clothes. No one is to know there was a death. Questions need not be raised."

I fidgeted with my sleeve. It was the ultimate betrayal, to ask me to remove my mourning clothes, as though we were less than acquaintances.

"I am obliged," I finally managed to say as I took the roll of bills.

Jonathan bowed and left the room. I would have wept, but I was wont even for tears.

Chapter Twenty-four

I found myself alone at my father's casket. It was yet dark, as I had risen before dawn to bid him farewell in privacy. I could not tell my feelings then; there was only emptiness inside, and try as I might I could think of nothing to utter. I sat in the room for a fair interval before making my way back to the chamber, in case the dead was watching from the spirit world.

I gathered my things and penned Jonathan a note indicating I would contact him from London. I knew he would not be along to see me off, and further that he would not be anxious to hear from me again, but I felt it was the proper thing to do. I left the note with the butler when at last he came to escort me to the carriage prepared for me.

At Leechman's, it was easy to feel tempted to exploit Jonathan's generosity by purchasing loads of merchandise.

Nevertheless, I came out of the store with the two approved dresses, a hat, a new pair of boots, a shawl and a small trunk. It still felt indulgent, as the items were of very good quality. Who knew when I would have the means to purchase such things again? What I selected may need to service me for quite some time. Besides, I intended to command as much respect as possible from my new employer.

At the train station I opened the letter containing my instructions. My new employer's name was Mr. Charles Francis, and he dealt in fine women's wear. My duties and where I would be staying were not included in the letter. I hoped the working and living conditions would be decent. I would be sure to be very cautious indeed with what money Jonathan afforded me.

I found a bench near my platform and made myself at ease. I was informed by an attendant that the train was delayed, so I wandered across the street and into a small shop. There were on display all manner of small treasures, figurines, pocket watches, trinkets of gold. I lifted a beautiful crystal rose up to the window's light. As I did so, I saw a flash of blonde locks out of the corner of my eye.

There beyond the window glass was Isabella Davis. She must have just arrived, no doubt to attend my father's funeral, I surmised by her all-black attire. Had she come to hold Jonathan's hand as he grieved? What of my hand? I imagined the Madam at the side of the casket as well, a supposed pillar of community support for the bereaved.

Dare I intercept Isabella? In any case, the arrival of her train signaled that mine would surely be readying to take to the tracks. I must take the chance of a run in if I were to make my train. I set the figurine down and walked through the shop doors just as the Madam's carriage pulled up before Isabella.

"How do you do, Miss Davis?" I greeted as I passed, holding my head high. I did not stop to hear her reply, if there was to be one; I simply brushed past her like a brisk autumn wind. When I turned to look I saw that her jaw had dropped and her face was crimson. Beyond her I saw the Madam's profile in the window of the carriage.

So they were aware of my situation. How long had she and Jonathan been conversing during my exile? How had I not considered the scheme? I had not thought Jonathan capable, but now the insult was complete. So the knife reaches beyond the grave, and disease is perpetuated throughout the generations.

I knew what I had done would be enough to haunt Isabella. From then on I determined that my life would be in my hands alone. Mr. Charles Francis would not be receiving his new employee that afternoon. I could only imagine what sort of surprises they all had in store for me there.

"Pardon me, sir, I would like to exchange my ticket for another destination," I told the balding man behind the ticket desk.

"Where does your ticket take you?"

"To London, only I no longer wish to go there. I would far rather take a train elsewhere."

"The London train is boarding now. I cannot make an exchange on such short notice. Perhaps a refund, and you can come back tomorrow."

I stood considering this. I *could* get on the train just then and find my way through London. Or perhaps I should not be hasty in my choice of destination. Maybe I should lodge in town for the night and consider my options.

"Yes, tomorrow," I agreed. "Good day, sir."

He nodded his head impatiently and craned his neck to see who would be helped after me.

I would not need the services of a cab, as a lodging house lay just up the road. Once there I was unsure of how to handle myself; this was my first experience hiring a room, and I knew that doing so unescorted would bring me no esteem, but what choice did I have? I had an explanation at the ready in case I was asked—a lie, really, that my brother would be joining me later on—but the frowning, bespectacled gentleman at the desk did not probe me for information. Perhaps his mind was made up about the sort of woman I was. After handing over what I considered to be a small fortune, I was shown to my room.

"This should do for your—needs," the man said with a surly smile. He tipped his hat and walked in the opposite direction. His insinuation was lost on me.

I entered the tiny abode and looked 'round. In it was a small bed, a side table, and a secretary's desk with a chair. I closed the door and went immediately to the corner fireplace to start some kindling. It was, after all, the middle of winter. I sat on the bed: a straw mattress. Somehow I would need to come up with a plan for myself.

I had seen the clock at the front desk, which marked only noon. I could find an occupation there in town, or, I could take my ticket to London the following morning. London held a myriad of possibilities. The rumours of what could go amiss in such a large city, most especially to an unescorted lady such as myself, deterred me from this decision.

I could also make my way back to Hazel Grove. I would not be afforded the luxury of going home to Mother, but at least I could find a place to lodge nearby until I decided what to do next. I could still talk to Mother, couldn't I? I was sure I could convince Mrs. Bunting at the Post or someone else to oblige me for at least a few days. I could call on Mr. Roeing—but no.

I lay down. My head was beginning to ache and a new wave of anger toward Jonathan was threatening to take me under. Then I knew what to do. Quickly, I changed into my mourning clothes. What right had any of them to keep me from the funeral? What could they do, have me thrown out? I was sure they wouldn't, not in a public gathering.

It took no time at all to acquire a cab. Only one other coach made its way down the winding lane to Longhurst, the rest had already arrived. I hoped my entrance would not be noticeable. I exited and promised the driver a large tip if he would await me, for I was unsure how long I would be. I followed closely behind the other latecomers, an older man and his wife, in hopes I could be considered a part of their company.

In the room where my father lay, a religious service was under way. The butler was there to seat us near the back of the room. I was fortunate that my new black hat had on it a thin veil with which to cloak my eyes. I was able to pass before him unnoticed.

Once seated, I tensed and began to question my decisions. Did I have the fortitude to show my face to Jonathan and the Madam, or would I cower behind my veil as I had for the butler? I saw them all near the casket, Isabella practically weeping as she held to Jonathan's arm, moving her black lace-trimmed handkerchief from eye to eye. *She is feigning*, I thought. Jonathan was resolute as always, but his eyes were wetted. Watching them together there felt as if I were stealing glances into an ulterior reality, another dimension that I could not touch.

As everyone bowed their head to pray, I used the opportunity to scan over the crowd. I knew few of the people. Many of them I had seen at my grandfather's own funeral. Suddenly my stomach lurched as though it were being torn from my body.

I knew that profile, and the profile beside him. What on earth? Why had Mr. Roeing come, and with Lady Bristol? He turned his head so slightly in my direction that I was unsure if he had seen me, or even recognized me.

This I had not expected. Was Mr. Roeing a part of my brother's web in all of this? Was he, too, using me? Or was he only being a member of the club? My mind hurriedly attempted to piece it all together.

As soon as the prayer was ended and the minister made the announcement that the party should proceed to the burial ground, I stood and promptly made my way toward the door. It had been a mistake to attend. I walked as quickly as I could to my cab without drawing attention to myself.

I shouted my orders to the driver as I pushed open the leather accordion door and clambered inside the tiny compartment. I didn't care if it looked vulgar or un-ladylike, or that I should have hired a more spacious crawler for propriety's sake. I kept my head facing away from the manor as the crowd trickled out.

The cab did not move, and I grew anxious as I watched the carriages moving forward to block the pathway. Just as I was about to open the roof hatch to question the driver about the delay, someone pushed open the door opposite me.

Chapter Twenty-five

"And where would you be flitting off to just now, Miss Thurgood?" Mr. Roeing asked as he peeked his head into the cab.

I turned my head away in anger. He slid in beside me and closed his door as the cab pulled forward.

"What do you think you're doing?" I asked without turning.

"Why, I'm hitching a ride. I hope you won't begrudge me."

"I am not sure that I do or do not," I said. "But I would appreciate a donation toward the fare if you insist on hitching."

Mr. Roeing laughed. "All spit and fire. Don't worry; I've already made my contribution to the driver." He grew more serious. "I thought you were away."

"You mean you *hoped* I was away?"

"No. Though I must say how impressed I am. I was unsure whether you would have the gall to make an appearance today."

"What of Lady Bristol?"

"I sent her ahead of me. There won't be much time to discuss."

"Discuss? Are you part of this entanglement as well? Is that how you always seem to know things?"

He pulled the curtain closed on his window, then reached over me to close mine. Sharing the tiny space with him felt risky, sacrilegious.

I listened to him explain why he had come. He had been invited, as he had known my father casually. The Madam and Jonathan indeed were part of a conspiracy, a ploy to keep my father's sins undercover, and their reputations unblemished. I was the spoiler. Isabella was more or less an innocent pawn. She did not have the backbone to displease her grandmother by interceding on my behalf.

I wasn't sure I believed him. I told him of Jonathan's arrangements for me in London, and that I had refused to follow along.

"You did well. I doubt whatever plans they had for you were to your benefit. You have grown in your understanding of things."

224

"Mr. Roeing, with respect, I am confused about your intentions here. You are always rearing your head into my affairs. Now that I know you are a duke, I can't see why any of this is consequential to you."

"Listen very carefully. I am sending you to Oxford. There is a widow there that will take you in. She will need an assistant in her watch repair shop. The pay is low, but all your needs will be met. It will be good for you there. Take the train to Oxford and hire a cab to take you to the south end and to the Widow Donovan. Everyone knows where to find her."

"But what—?" I started as we neared the town centre. Mr. Roeing squeezed my hand.

"Remember, the Widow Donovan. I expect you'll send me a note at Roeing Oaks to tell me you've arrived. Now go! Lady Bristol will be suspicious if I keep her waiting any longer." He fairly pushed me from the cab. I watched as it took my dear Mr. Roeing away.

I stood on the curbside dumbfounded. At last I decided to go to the tea house Isabella had introduced me to and enjoy a light meal as I thought things over. As I sipped my tea and admired the artwork hanging on the walls, I imagined what kind of life I could have led with someone like Mr. Roeing, if only my father had not driven my mother away that evening so many years ago.

I thought of Mr. Roeing and his lady partaking of a good meal alongside my grieving kin while I sat alone. The entirety of the loss covered me like a lead sheath. I ate one scone too many and hid another in my pocket for the morning. If Mr. Roeing was not being true with me, I didn't know what I would do.

After wandering through the town for sometime feeling sorry for myself, I found my way back to the lodging house, where sleep came surprisingly easy. I was up at dawn and on my way to the train station. I boarded a train to Oxford.

AS INSTRUCTED, I HIRED A CAB to take me to the Widow Donovan. The driver agreed, with a strange expression. At the edge of the town centre, in an almost obscure corner, was the watch repair shop. It was non-descript with its brown roof tiles and small shop window, no different than those around it. Then again, it also appeared ethereal. I rapped on the door, and after a moment opened it cautiously and peeked my head in. I could see no one.

The room was sparse. There was the desk to the left, and straight ahead an array of watches was displayed in a glass case with various price tags attached to them. On the wall behind it was a cuckoo clock, but otherwise the walls were void of decorations. I had never seen a cuckoo clock, so when the bird popped out at the stroke of the hour I let out a yelp.

"Who's there?" I heard a firm, deep, female voice call from somewhere beyond the room. As she peeped out through a door at the back of the room, I caught my first glance of the Widow Donovan. One never forgot their first glance of the Widow. Her hair was black, jet black, and she wore it partly down, unheard of in those days for a woman of her age. Her eyes were sound; that is, there was no fright or concern in them. She wore black as well, and I couldn't help thinking she gave the overall effect of a witch. She looked me over quickly.

"Katherine," she stated.

"Mr.—he sent me here," I stuttered. I was unsure of what to call him, Mr. Roeing, or His Grace? She nodded her head in understanding. I was relieved not to be questioned further on the matter.

"This way," she said and she disappeared to a room in the back. I left my belongings behind the desk and followed. In the back room were a stove, a table, two chairs, and another desk.

I did not see the Widow there so I ventured into an adjoining room, where I found her standing beside a hutch containing plates and bowls, a bureau, and a straw mattress barely elevated above the ground by what appeared to be a

227

wooden pallet. The mattress was covered in a worn patch quilt—the only colourful object to be found.

"You will sleep here," she said. I noted the narrow staircase not far from the mattress. "That is where I stay. You are not to go there."

"Yes, madam," I answered. She looked me over yet again. I averted my eyes.

"Wages are small, but food won't be scarce. You'll be responsible for most of the cooking and caretaking. I can see you have a detailed eye. You should have no trouble with watch work." I nodded, wondering how in a few glances she could have surmised as much about me.

"And now go and fetch some potatoes for dinner at the market; a few leeks as well. At the end of the road turn right. You can't miss it." She handed me a basket and a few coins before disappearing up the steps.

I did as I was instructed and walked to the market, which was further away than suggested. As always in winter there were fewer vendors than otherwise, and it did not take long to find potatoes. I gathered several into the basket and prepared to pay the heavyset lady with the rosy cheeks behind the cart. I could not help but inquire about the Widow. Mr. Roeing had said everyone knew of her.

"Pardon me, I wonder what you can tell me of the Widow Donovan?"

"The Widow Donovan! What do you need to know of 'at witch?" She leaned in closer. "She murdered 'er 'usband, y' know," she whispered, her face distorting with the pleasure of gossip. "Everyone knows it. He died in 'is prime. Never 'armed a man in all 'is blessed days. She got to 'im, she did."

"Wh-what happened?"

"Oh, no one can prove it. But she keeps to 'erself like an 'ermit, and me don't trust 'ermits. Mr. Donovan was a right cheerful man, straight from Dublin; made a name for 'imself 'ere. Methinks she did it for 'is money, but some thinks she did it for a dark ritual, if ya know what I'm gettin' at."

"Was he quite wealthy?" I asked.

"A man needn't be wealthy to be a target for a greedy soul," she said, sucking in her cheeks and giving a knowing look.

"I see. Thank you," I said. I paid her and started back. I couldn't make any sense out of it. What would Mr. Roeing have to do with a witch or a murderer? I decided to keep it all in my heart and decide for myself over time if I believed such a report. After purchasing some leeks, I set back for the watch repair shop.

Inside, I did not see the Widow. On the table beside a loaf of bread was a note with instructions to prepare potato and leek cakes and tea.

I set about preparing the meal. My days of delicate cuisine and handmaidens were over. It seemed it had been a year or more since I last cooked, but in reality it had only been months. I looked at my softened hands and sighed.

In the midst of stoking the fire in the stove, I heard a creaking noise above me. She was there. Everything I had heard at the market jumped about in my mind. Did she wish to kill me, too? What if Mr. Roeing was sending me to my death as a favour to my family? I shook my head to rid myself of the thought. As if on cue, she appeared exactly as dinner was completed.

"Good afternoon," I greeted. A nod was returned me. She set the table for two. She bowed her head and recited a blessing for the food before sitting down. Not long into our meal, I broke the unbearable silence.

"Pardon me, Mrs. Donovan, but if you don't mind my asking, I wonder if you could tell me how it is you know Mr.— well, His Grace?"

The Widow guffawed. "Did he call himself Mr. Roeing for you, too?" she asked, obviously amused.

"Yes."

"I'm not one who enjoys conversation, but this you will need to know. The Duke came upon my shop a while back under the name Mr. Roeing. I suppose that is where you come in."

"I don't understand."

She blinked, then swallowed her food. "You could call us relation. My brother was Earnest Thurgood."

Chapter Twenty-six

I coughed up a mouthful of food. It isn't everyday one meets with an estranged family member, but for me it was becoming commonplace.

"I suppose the Duke will wish to know you've arrived safely. You may go tomorrow and make a telegram to him, as well as to your mother. How is she?"

I grasped the table. "Do you *know* my mother?"

"No, but I know the story. My brother was a good man."

"Y-you don't resemble him. Not that I recall his features explicitly."

"Explicitly—marvelous word," she said, her eyes misting over. She seemed lost in another world for a moment, and then all at once she was with me again. "If you mean my hair, I dye it. Gives people something to chat about, keeps them from venturing into my business."

"Don't you want them to venture into your business?" I asked.

She laughed. "I wasn't speaking of the repair shop. I'm a secretive old woman is all." I didn't perceive her as old in the least. She was very much alive, and striking. "The Duke told me all. For now you will abide here. There is much to teach you."

I did not have the presence of mind to ask what sort of things I would need be taught, and she did not seem to have the patience to speak with me further. Her mind was elsewhere, and soon after dinner she put a "closed" sign on the door and again disappeared up the stairs. I could see I would have to garner the information in installments.

I was grateful that my training began in watch work immediately so that I would not have the time to dwell on my circumstances. I found my training confusing, though in a few weeks my hands grew steadily more deft, and my spirits lifted. As well I scrubbed the floors, cooked, washed the laundry, fetched, and naturally ran myself ragged in a manner I was no longer accustomed to. In it all I noticed a baffling pattern.

The Widow would leave me to keep shop in the mornings for an hour while she went out, to where I did not know. During that hour, one customer may meander into the shop, and I knew that she could not be getting many more business throughout the day. In her free time she secluded herself upstairs. I began to wonder how it was that she was making enough of a living to feed herself and pay me as well. Perhaps Mr. Roeing was giving her a stipend to house me.

One day the Widow motioned to me to follow her up the enigmatic stairwell that I was told never to use. The rumors I had heard about town roused themselves in my mind. Was this where she took her victims before slaying them? I laughed at my own absurd fears and proceeded cautiously up the creaky steps.

What was dull and drab on the first level of the shop was of most notable contrast to the second. I stood there absorbing it all. There was colour here, and life. The walls were covered in French toile paper, its signature black and white scenes the perfect backdrop for the fresh green secretary's desk and the pale pink bureau that was splashed with hand painted floral artwork. There were several bookcases stuffed to the brim with books. The bed at the far end of the room was decked in soft fabrics that began at the ceiling and softly draped around the tufted black headboard.

I looked at the Widow in surprise. She motioned me to the desk.

"You are ready, I have found you trustworthy. Read this," she said, handing me a sheet of paper from one of the many tall stacks atop the desk. It was a lecture from what I could tell, something one might read at a school. Its author was Earnest Carrington. I looked to her for further explanation.

"What do you think of it?" she asked.

"Well, I—" I wasn't sure what I was expected to think.

"It's some of my best work, and you can think of nothing to say about it?" I looked down again at the paper. I could not find her name anywhere on the page.

"You won't find it there. Haven't you ever heard of a pen name?"

I had not.

"Watch work is what my husband did, and I keep the shop, mostly so that I have an excuse to stay in town. My real profession is writing. I write lectures for some of the professors at the university, and for that I cannot attach my own name to it or it won't be taken seriously. So I use a male pen name. I am fortunate enough to make something of an income at it, but my true love is poetry.

"Why are you allowing me to see all this?"

"Because you are a writer, too." I wondered how she could know such a thing. *I* did not know it.

Over the next few weeks in addition to my chores, my new assignments were based in writing. As I did them, I felt more in place than ever. As I practiced my new craft and read the works the Widow placed before me, I felt alive. She was no witch. She was an artist, and I admired her.

One thing served to dampen my spirits. It was the reaction I garnered each time I went out in public. I knew what they were all thinking of me, staying with the mysterious woman. My heart ached that all the beauty she had to offer was squelched by a mere supposition. How many more out there were victims of supposition? Yet she had found a way to give of herself, even without merit.

"I've found this among my things," the Widow said to me one day.

It was a photo of Earnest, the man I once called my father. The photo was taken long before Mother and I came into his world. He looked content. It brought me a great sense of him, and I would keep it next to my bed the remainder of my stay there, right beside the oak tree from Joseph, the letter from Mother, and the bottle of perfume that Mr. Roeing had given me. These were mementos of all the people in the world that ever loved me.

One afternoon as I was writing the beginning of an intense poem, I was interrupted.

"It will soon be May you know," the Widow said.

"Yes, I can hardly believe it's nearly here. I adore May," I answered absentmindedly.

"Katherine, how is your progress?"

"It is you I should be asking."

"I was referring to you personally. Where do you see yourself heading?"

I set down my pen. "Are you hinting at something?"

She handed me an invitation, the one to Mr. Roeing's engagement ball. I sighed, put it down and returned to my work.

"Yes, I know of it. I was given one as well."

"You must go."

Instead of asking her why I searched her eyes. "Are you telling me you wish for me to leave you?

"My assignment is complete," she said quietly.

"Why? Have I not pleased you?" She laughed and reached out to stroke my hair. This was the first time she had touched me.

"I was asked to help you, and I did. You have helped me as well."

I stood and paced the room. "What has Mr. Roeing told you? Has he paid you to house me?"

The Widow blinked, but outside of this, no acknowledgement.

"In a few days I will bid you farewell at the train station. You will go alone. I have no desire to be party to such a grand event."

"But I—I have no gown."

"Then tell him so. I'm certain he would afford you one. Why don't you go a day early? That way you can discuss what you wish with him in privacy."

A few days later, in a numb state of mind, I found myself in transit to Roeing Oaks. I decided to do as the Widow suggested and go a day ahead of time so that I could say goodbye to Mr. Roeing in private.

"All the trees of the field will know that I the LORD bring down the tall tree and make the low tree grow tall. I dry up the green tree and make the dry tree flourish.
"'I the LORD have spoken, and I will do it.'"

Ezekiel 17:24

Chapter Twenty-seven

My heart swirled within me as I traveled beneath the canopy of oaks along the lane leading to the great white behemoth that was Roeing Oaks. The trees were laden with fresh green leaves that made the lane so much lovlier than the first time I had passed through it, and the landscaping ahead was filled with colourful new blooms in the most majestic shades. A few gardeners were scattered about, busied at clipping shrubbery and tending to the plantings.

When we had reached the bottom of the cascading staircase, I sat in the crawler contemplating what I should do next. The footman knocking at the window startled me so that I dropped the box in my hands. Thankfully, I had had the foresight to purchase a gift.

The footman opened the door and offered me his arm to steady my descent. I took a moment to speak to the cab driver.

"In one hour, if you please, return to the first bend in the road. If I am not there to meet you—here—take this, for your time." I handed him an extra bit of money.

I followed the footman up the great staircase. Through the windows I could see the servants busily preparing for the gala that would take place the following evening. When the door was opened to me, it was as if it had opened into a fairytale. Gads of candelabras and flowers overtook the foyer: peonies, snap dragons, the first of the roses of the season, soft and pink; even white lilies; and the scent was heavenly. Great strings of greenery adorned the staircase, golden ribbon threaded through it like fine embroidery. I was taken with its splendor.

"State your business," commanded the butler. I could see I was imposing on his duties. "A delivery?" he asked after seeing my box.

"Well, yes, a delivery for His Grace." He held out his hand to receive it.

"Oh, no, no. I—I was requested to deliver it in person. It comes from a dear friend, and I have a message."

"As you can imagine, His Grace is utterly preoccupied at the moment."

"I understand, and I promise not to occupy a mite more of his time than is necessary. Please? At least notify him?"

The butler overlooked me dubiously. "Whom may I tell him is calling?"

"Miss Katherine Thurgood. I don't have a calling card with me, but I've been here before," I stumbled.

"Wait here, Miss Thurgood. I cannot give you any indication His Grace will receive you." After several minutes the butler returned. "This way, miss." I was led down the familiar hallway that I had gone down in December, the one leading to Mr. Roeing's study. It took all the courage I had to step inside.

Upon seeing him, only nostalgia filled me. What was it about him that always set me at ease? Mr. Roeing was finishing some business with a man, and when he saw me his eyes lit up, though he was careful not to show it until his associate had exited the room. When he had closed the door he eagerly embraced me. This I had not planned to have to react to.

"Kate," he whispered giddily. "You've arrived early!"

Again, his nearness, his piney aftershave, his penetrating eyes; I was at a loss for words. Wasn't he supposed to be too frenzied with last minute details to take time with me? Now he had me by the hands. "Come, sit," he urged.

I obeyed.

"Darling, you look wretched! Did the Widow neglect to feed you or give you rest? What is the matter? Here, I have some tea and biscuits, if you don't mind sharing my cup." He picked it up and wiped the edge with a handkerchief before pouring tea.

"Thank you," I said, accepting the tea. I handed him the box in return. "For you and your lady. It's terribly delicate and it may not live long, I'm afraid, but when I saw it in the shop it seemed the purest gift. It reminded me of, ahem, love," I croaked, unable to say the word forthrightly.

He opened the box and beheld the exotic purple orchid that I had used a good portion of my money to purchase. He exclaimed how beautiful it was and thanked me for my thoughtfulness. In the ensuing silence his eyes darted about for an instant.

"Kate, is there a reason you've arrived ahead of time?"

"I wanted to—to speak with you in private. I—well I don't have anything to wear to such a splendid event. I would feel ashamed to attend in something as plain as this," I said, motioning to my dress, my best. "I didn't wish to put anyone out. And I thought it best to speak with you now, before your mind is harried with all the guests and things. The Widow said I won't be going back to her so I have no idea what I am to do."

Suddenly the dam that had so faithfully withheld my tears burst into thousands of ragged pieces. I began to sob, feeling even more the fool.

"Darling, you mustn't worry a fig about anything. I am so happy you have come!" He gave me a moment to collect myself. "Do not fret. I've planned a special surprise for you. Would you like to see it?" he asked, tipping my chin up so that our eyes would meet. I nodded, though I truly wished to dart toward the door.

With his signature tenderness, he took me by the hand and led me along to a suite.

"Let us see what this room possesses," he said with a mischievous grin.

Upon entering, I was so taken aback at the brilliance of the room itself that I did not notice the exquisite ball gown laid out upon the curtained bed.

"What is this?" I asked in amazement.

"Of course I knew you would not have a gown. And you should be aware by now that I overlook nothing." He looked at his watch. "But this is only one of the surprises. The other is for after dinner. I expect you will be my dinner guest, and what a pleasant surprise for me." He absentmindedly touched my hair.

"But I've nothing to wear—to dinner, that is."

"Come, you are lovely as you are," he said as he held his arm out to me. I thought of Lady Bristol for an instant, that she ought to be having dinner with him in my place, but I banished the thought. She was sure to be busy readying herself. She probably hadn't yet arrived from her own estate.

We ate alone in an informal dining area tucked away in a wing of the manor I had not been to. We carried on as old friends are known to, our memories comforting us like a mink coat. I would not allow myself to think that this was the last time I would see him that way. I began to ask him for advice on what I should do next with myself. He only put his finger to his lips.

"There will be a time for that, but now is time for something else." He set down his fork and his napkin and stood to help me up from my chair.

"Come this way." He was leading me back to the extraordinary suite containing the gown. Suddenly I began to perspire. I had read about this sort of thing. Did he have intentions? If he did all respect I had for him would be lost. Perhaps he wished me to be his—no!

"Are you well?" he asked.

"Yes. I am only anticipating what could be next," I said, trying to smile. I felt his hand at the small of my back. I noticed a servant girl further down the hall, saw the question in her eyes. My anxiety swelled. Had she seen this before? Was this his custom? What of Lady Bristol? As much as I cared for him I would be no mistress! As we stopped at the door I prepared to assert myself. He smiled and motioned for me to open the door.

"Sir, I cannot!"

"Would you prefer that I open the door?" he asked with a laugh. He knocked once.

The door swung open.

Kristina Emmons

I staggered at what, or rather who, I found on the other side.

"Mother!" I cried.

Chapter Twenty-eight

Mother and I embraced for a long while. Her arms were home.
It had been nearly six months since we had been together.

"I will leave the two of you to reacquaint," I heard Mr.
Roeing say.

"Wait! Not yet!" I walked to him and wrapped my arms
around him. "Thank you, from the bottom of my heart," I
whispered in his ear. I held to him a little longer than may be
appropriate, but I felt at home there as well. Then I pulled back,
and smiling, kissed his hand. "You are amazing, sir."

He returned the smile and disappeared down the
corridor.

There was so much to say, and Mother and I took no
measures to withhold any of it. We chatted on into the early
hours of the morning, a parallel to the night that the letter had
arrived in Hazel Grove, but with far more gaiety.

Mother told me how she and Joseph were getting along, and how she was enjoying being housekeeper to the new tenants at Chatworthy House. She was dressed well enough, and she appeared content. For this my own happiness was increased a thousand fold.

"Mother, how long have you known that Mr. Roeing was the Duke of Berkshire?"

"When last he visited at Christmas he revealed himself. I was not surprised. I knew there was something unusual concerning him. What a pleasing revelation," she said, motioning to our surroundings. "It is good to have friends in high places."

"Oh, look! There is a gown for you as well!" I exclaimed. Mother put her hands to her head in disbelief.

"This will be the most memorable gathering of your life. Just look at the detailing in the gowns!" she exclaimed.

"Will this be the last gathering of its kind for us?"

"I suppose. Let us pretend it is true to life. Tomorrow we will strut as princesses and forget—all that is to be forgotten."

"We have one another," I said.

In the morning breakfast was delivered to our suite and we leisurely enjoyed the morning as the sounds of the preparations echoed beneath us. After, as Mother napped, her face overcome with a soft expression, I pondered. Really I was wont to prepare myself for the coming heartbreak as Mr. Roeing chose his love publicly.

After some time, I came to the realization that I didn't need all the grandeur to bring me happiness. I had everything that constituted true wealth: health, the love of those around me, the understanding of who I was. All else were unnecessary frills. If Hazel Grove were my fate, so be it. If scullery maid was my fate, though I would dread it, so be it.

I felt I would no longer need private conference with Mr. Roeing. I could make this next decision on my own. He had been so good to help us, but it was time to let him go. I would return home with Mother and face what was in store for me. I breathed deeply, maybe for the first time in months.

There were ladies in waiting assigned to us to ready us for the ball. When they were finished with us we looked like a pair of sister princesses. It was so good to see Mother this way, the way she was meant to be. Now I could see the source of Aunt Betina's jealousy.

Just as we were about to be escorted to the ballroom we were arrested by the ladies in waiting. There was yet one more gift—exquisite jewelry to befit our gowns. For me, a choker with an emerald center stone, and for mother, rubies.

We made our way through the foyer, where we obtained our dance cards. Mother and I seemed to be gaining attention already. I noticed a gentleman with a monocle staring rather forthrightly at Mother. I giggled.

We peeked into the dining hall we were overcome by the perfume emanating from the thousands of flowers. Each of the dozens of tables was ethereally draped in tulle and flowers and silver candelabras. The soft glow created by the candlelight was unforgettably romantic. There were even ribbons and flowers floating from above like heavenly beings, suspended carefully so that they were close enough to be admired, yet far enough from reach that they could not be tampered with. Twisted in amongst them were delicate Venetian glass balls.

Everyone was dressed in the finest they could rally, and jewels were as plenteous as the flowers. Our enjoyment was only beginning. There, at the far end of the foyer, stood Queen Victoria herself! She wore a diamond-encrusted tiara, which blazed as the sun against her black mourning attire. Since the death of her husband, Prince Albert, several years earlier, she had not been seen in anything but black, and from her countenance I could see that she mourned him still.

Just before the ballroom were tables filled with hors d'oeuvres such as foie gras, delicate meats, kumquats, pineapples, jellies, and there was no shortage of champagne! But Mr. Roeing was nowhere to be found. An announcement was made that we should proceed to the ballroom. My heart twisted within. Was this the moment of the announcement? It was not. There would first be music and dance.

We sneaked past the announcer and into the ballroom.

I was stunned to find one Mr. Thomas Remington in our midst. I turned to Mother to tell her who it was, and to ask for advice. "Let us walk nearby and see what his reaction will be. Pretend you do not see him!" she urged.

"Why, Miss Katherine Thurgood!" Mr. Remington exclaimed when he saw me. He bowed.

"How do you do, Mr. Remington?" I greeted with a curtsy, attempting at charm and innocence.

"I must say I was disappointed that we had to break our meeting, though it seems fate has intervened. And who is this lovely lady serving as your escort?"

"Allow me to introduce you to my mother, Lady Thurgood." I was elevating her rank, I knew, but I didn't want any questions asked. He bowed and kissed her hand.

"Would you allow me the honour, Lady Thurgood, of escorting your daughter to a dance?"

"My daughter would be enchanted to dance with so dashing a gentleman." And with a wink from Mother I was promptly swept up into dance. We swirled effortlessly through a waltz, and after he wrote his name in my dance card.

I could not find Mother. At last I saw her dancing with a fine gentleman, and clearly enjoying herself. I laughed in spite of myself. Next I danced with a Spanish man, whose dark eyes were magnetic, and by which I intended to avoid being captured. I reunited with Mother just in time for the Duke's entrance.

The crowd parted to either side of the ballroom to make way for the official entrance of the Duke of Berkshire. After everyone bowed and he had made his way to the head of the room, the music again commenced. I looked to Mother for some sort of cue. She motioned to continue as normal. I decided to get a drink of punch for us.

This is when I first noticed Jonathan and Isabella. I hurried to tell Mother, who appeared pallid.

"Your grandmother is here, Kate!" she whispered, breathless.

"And Jonathan with Isabella!" We looked about and decided it was best to cross to the opposite end of the room.

Where was Mr. Roeing? There, there he was. And the others? It was suddenly pertinent that I be invisible. What purpose did Mr. Roeing have in inviting our mortal enemies?

"Is something the matter, Miss Thurgood? You look positively faint," Thomas asked.

"I *am* feeling faint. I suppose I could use a bit of fresh air. Do you mind?" He took my cue and escorted me to the veranda, safely away from the drama. I motioned to Mother that she follow us.

"I must confess, I had rather be somewhere with you where we can exchange conversation," Thomas said. "You look stunning this evening."

"I say she does, and what a surprise to find her here," said Jonathan. Isabella clung dutifully to his arm.

At my bristling, Thomas stepped in. "Pardon me, are you acquainted with Miss Thurgood?"

"Yes, we are acquainted," I said. "This is my brother, Mr. Jonathan Percy, and my cousin, Miss Isabella Davis. Have you made Mr. Remington's acquaintance, Jonathan?"

I knew I had angered Jonathan in introducing him as my brother. He ignored my introduction.

"Katherine, my dear friend in London desires to know what has become of you." He reached over and fingered my choker. "Wherever did you acquire such a dud?"

Thomas looked from Jonathan to me, not knowing how to broach the situation. Isabella stepped aside and fidgeted with her silk fan. I saw her décolletage reddening, the flame traveling all the way up to her face.

"I don't suppose it's important. Nor any of your business," I answered coolly. "Please excuse us, Jonathan, Mr. Remington and I have reserved a dance."

Jonathan took me by the elbow. Thomas stepped in and put his hand on Jonathan's arm. He ignored the interception.

"How dare you speak to me so! I demand to know how it is you came here!" Jonathan spat.

"Good evening, Mr. Percy," Mother said calmly from behind him. She had squared her shoulders as was her custom, and her jade eyes were glowing with dare. Jonathan's eyes darted between the two of us, attempting to piece together a reason for our collective presence.

"I would enjoy a stroll with you just now, Katherine," Jonathan said.

"You will have no such opportunity," Mother answered. "She and Mr. Remington are excused so that you and *I* may have an exchange."

Thomas promptly escorted me away, and into a waltz. I kept watch of the party as we swirled. Thomas was rigid.

"Is there something you wish to explain to me, Miss Thurgood?" he asked.

Where was Mr. Roeing? I could not seem to place him. Had he seen what just happened?

"I suppose I should explain, yet I don't foresee that I can at this time. Please, let us enjoy the dance." I could see that Jonathan and Isabella had moved on, and that the Madam was standing with Mother, who was clearly uncomfortable. I longed to hear the conversation between them. Where had Mr. Roeing gone? Ah, there, there to the side, joyously conversing with a grandly dressed man. Did he not see?

When Jonathan and Isabella had gotten a little too close to us as they danced, I asked Thomas to escort me to the side. I saw that Mother now stood alone. I curtseyed and thanked Mr. Remington. He tentatively took his exit.

I took Mother by the hand. "Come, we've endured enough." But my tugging was met with resistance.

"It's all right, Kate. I'm fine."

"Why should we stay, Mother? Don't you see? It was all a trap. This Mr. Roeing, or the Duke, or whatever he is; he is inwardly cruel. No kind person would put us through it. And now any chance I might have had with Mr. Remington is likely ruined."

"Mr. Roeing is not cruel. We will stay."

I shook my head. "I cannot. Please, if you would stay until the announcement, meet me outside after."

As I looked up my eyes met with Mr. Roeing's. His eyes pierced me, searched me; they knew me. I was convinced I would live my life through and never find eyes like those again. They were my devastation.

I walked to the entryway leading to the foyer. Just then the servants began closing the doors.

"Wait! I must get through!" I cried.

"No one is to exit at this time. His Grace is about to make the official announcement."

255

"But I need to—" The doors closed with a thud. I put my hand to my brow and lowered my head. I heard the music stop and the crowd beginning to chatter. A dozen or more servants set about passing flutes filled with champagne to each guest. I stood there, lost. I could no longer see Mother.

The crowd parted as the Red Sea, leaving a narrow walkway between them, and I was urged to step off to one side as well, a champagne flute having also been transferred into my hand. I closed my eyes, breathed; remembered the days before the letter had arrived. I was content then, wasn't I? Everything had been so simple. What was life but a series of mornings and evenings, and seed times and harvests, peppered with laughter and tears?

I could no longer hide the truth from myself. What I had known was not life, but existence. I could have passed another fifty years in that rotting cottage, allowing the world to pulse around me without ever daring to wonder what my part was in it. I would have faded with the seasons as a leaf before its descent into death.

And now? What now? I smelled destiny on the wind. I wasn't sure where my foot would step next, but I allowed the fingers of the unknown to grip me, and the sensation was one of rabid fear. I was willing to go where life would take me.

After a formal introduction, I opened my eyes to see Mr. Roeing take his place, the Queen of England flanking him. He scanned the audience, cleared his throat.

"Ladies and gentleman, I wish to express my gratitude for joining with me on this most important occasion. Your presence is a bolster to me, and my pleasure. I have no intentions of disappointing you this evening, but I'm afraid my announcement is not the one you have been led to expect."

The crowd groaned, questioning one another.

"Lady Bristol and I have come to an understanding with one another. In this world where marriages are arranged for convenience and power, I have found in her someone to love. But as many of you know, I am about to embark on a charitable mission in Africa that will take the better part of a year. Therefore, we have decided to postpone our ultimate decision."

A soft roar of wonderment swept through the gathering like a strengthening wind. I could see them craning their necks to find Lady Bristol, but she was not to be found.

"This past Season I was absent from all its events, even my favorite: the regatta. As this is something of a mystery, allow me to explain how I have occupied my time."

I could not find my breath. Where was Mother?

"Beginning in March I took a sabbatical to a hamlet in Northampton. You see, I decided to try an experiment. How many of us in Society know the plight of the common man?

What is it like to be the foreman of a farm? I intended to find out. So I came upon a landowner and convinced him to give me the office." The crowd laughed in disbelief.

"That's right, I spent the growing season living as a common man, and I enjoyed most every minute of it. And I had the assistance of two wonderful ladies that served as my housemaids. Where are you, Miss Katherine Thurgood? Mrs. Victoria Thurgood?" He searched through the crowd.

I was rooted in place.

"Come! It's all right," he reassured when he spotted us. As the audience parted for us, we met up and walked toward him, clasping each other's hands when at last we met. I felt the eyes of the people penetrating me. I forced Mother to stand beside Mr. Roeing, and I clung to her on the other side.

"These are the ladies I spent a good deal of time with there in the country. Surely you are confused as to why I have invited them here, of all places. Well, I have a secret concerning them. Once upon a time, as they say, someone very close to them did something wretched against them, causing them to be disinherited, as it were. We are here today to make it right." Mother and I exchanged expressions of shock, then looked to Mr. Roeing.

"You see, Mrs. Thurgood comes from a very prominent family in the kingdom, and she married someone of nobility—a name you no doubt have heard. While pregnant, she was banished from her home by her selfish husband, whose name I will not forbear, out of respect for his recent passing. He then invented insidious rumours about her and spread them around so that she could have no hope of reconciliation."

By now the crowd had ceased their murmuring and stood still to hear the story.

"You would never guess from how beautiful they look tonight, but for the past eighteen years these ladies have been made to live in poverty, and even now their own blood refuses to offer them grace, for their good name is far more important to them than the welfare of their kin. Tonight, I urge this family, before the Queen herself, that they give these ladies what is just—reinstatement.

"Let them therefore be regarded as ladies and no longer as part of the servant class. If the family does not welcome them as such, the whole truth of their case will be published throughout the kingdom, though I fear the truth will publish itself as a testimony against them. Out of pity, I will not call your names."

I dared raise my head to search for my family. I saw the shadow of horror on their faces and felt their shame. But my relief was that Mr. Roeing did not turn out to be one of them. His kindness was pure, after all. He looked at me, smiled.

"And now, do not be sorrowful that I have not made an engagement. Let us celebrate love and charity! Cheers!"

The audience clinked their champagne flutes together in salutation before draining them. Even the Queen clapped her hands. The music began again, and the floor was overtaken with a rainbow of swirling gowns; except for three very solemn people, who stood as statues until deciding to depart.

Mr. Roeing addressed us. "There is someone whose acquaintance you should make." As we were led to the Queen, we bowed in reverence. She had no words, only that queenly nod I had heard about, but I read mercy on her face, and I was at ease. I wondered how much of our situation she had been told.

"And now, Kate, may I be honoured to have your hand in this dance?" Mr. Roeing asked with a bow and an extended hand.

He'd said my name differently, not the way he had always addressed me. It was more intimate; my name spoken from the lips of a close friend and not a master. To call him by his Christian name in return was still too risky, as it would have indicated more intimacy between us than I understood us to have.

"Of course I will dance; I thought you would never ask," I said with a smile. As we turned about the room, I imagined I was royalty.

"This is all for you, you know," Mr. Roeing whispered in my ear. "Call it a coming of age ball." I looked at him in question.

"Lady Bristol and I decided a long while ago we were to postpone, and if you were to know the truth, there will be no engagement. This is all for you."

"But I—I—don't," He put a finger to my lips.

"No need for words. Come, I have something to discuss with you." He escorted me past the dancers and into the foyer, then on through the castle until we'd reached a side entrance. At last we were outside and we descended the stairs. We walked past the perimeter of light cast from the manor and into the shadows, the sounds of celebration trailing behind us as a king's cloak.

"Walk with me," he said as we walked under the canopy of oak trees. He held my hand. *A perfect fit*, I thought. We walked along to the beat of my thumping heart for several paces before stopping. Mr. Roeing turned to face me.

"Kate, I will be going away to Africa as I said, but I wondered if while I was away you and your mother wouldn't mind staying here at Roeing Oaks. And perhaps during that time you could try your hand at something new."

"What sort of something?" I asked.

"You know my work is quite important to me. Progress cannot stop while I am away. It's the women and children in London who need help the most. I think you and I could work well together, don't you?"

I looked up at him.

"What are you asking me?"

"I am asking you to assist me. But there would be training, and it isn't for the faint of heart. You must know how to carry yourself both in Society and as a member of our organization, and you will see things you will wish you had not. Will you consider it?"

Didn't he know I would do anything to be at his side?

"Yes!" I cried without hesitation. Relief washed over him.

"Yes?" he asked with a smile. I nodded in return, and we embraced. This time I did not intend to let go. I had him; I felt I really had him. Did he feel it too? I shuddered as he stroked my back. I pulled away. Perhaps I wasn't ready for such emotions.

I looked up at him, his face so soft in the moonlight that filtered through the treetops. He cupped my face in his hands and kissed me tenderly. A fire rushed through me, an ember had burst into flame.

When it ended, I buried my head in his shoulder.

"I have wanted that for so long," he whispered as he held me close.

"And I."

"Kate, look at me." I raised my head. He smiled.

"You look glorious."

I pointed to the emerald at my neck. "It must be this."

"No, it's you. It's all you. You are very beautiful, indeed, although you can keep the necklace. That is, if I can keep you." I beamed. He wrapped his arm around my waist and led me toward what was to be my new residence; at least for a time.

"Kate, what about this Thomas Remington you've been keeping company with? Do you fancy him?"

I laughed. "Oh, Mr. Roeing! He's a poor substitute for the Duke of Berkshire."

"Good, I've been stifling the urge to choke Mr. Remington all evening. And darling?"

"Hmm?"

"Call me Edward."

"All right then. Edward," I whispered.

When we reached the castle and had gone through the corridor, we put enough distance between us to appear publicly respectable. Then, side by side, we entered the dining hall.

The End

Acknowledgements

To my husband for his unwavering belief in me.

To Mom and Karyn Sigurdsson for their ongoing input and support during the writing of this book.

To Amanda Koziar, for her genius as a (cover) designer and for expertly navigating all my perfectionist whims.

To Jesus Christ, the Light of my life, and the true Mr. Roeing

Look for the sequel to Roeing Oaks in 2010!

For information please visit RoeingOaks.com.

www.ingramcontent.com/pod-product-compliance
Lightning Source LLC
Chambersburg PA
CBHW031105260626
47172CB00001B/229